T0070032

THE ULTIMATE

WIZARDING
WORLD

GUIDE TO
MAGICAL
STUDIES

A Comprehensive Exploration of
Hogwarts's Classes and Curriculum

A Magical Education
a Millennium in the Making

For more than 1,000 years, Hogwarts School of Witchcraft and Wizardry has championed the legacy of four of Britain's most gifted witches and wizards. As the premier magical institution of the United Kingdom, Hogwarts's curriculum distills the founders' collective knowledge into a mere seven years of schooling. Tackling its sprawling course schedule makes for a daunting task—you'd be tempted to resort to time travel to make every second count. Between learning to fly, handling human-shaped plants whose screams can dispatch even the most cunning wizards, confronting a creature that takes on your worst fears and much more, it's a wonder students don't lock themselves in their dormitories from the pressure of this impossible course load. To Harry Potter, though—someone who's no stranger to rooming in a cupboard under the stairs at his Muggle aunt and uncle's house—this ancient institution is the home he's always wanted, the place where he belongs. No matter how many parchments he's asked to write for History of Magic or how many Flobberworms he must sort through as part of his detention, Hogwarts is the unbreakable link to Harry's past and the key to his future. Well, just as soon as he pulls off top marks on his exams, anyway, and *Accio N.E.W.T.s* isn't going to help him there.*

For anyone curious to know the age at which you should be able to make an iguana vanish, which object to shove down your throat when you've been poisoned, what the deal is with those skeletal horses no one else seems to see or what color coat a unicorn has when it's a wobbly little foal, this book is for you. Alternatively, if you'd like to learn which Ministers of Magic had a hand in shaping Muggle history, what it takes to "stopper death" without resorting to alchemy (hint: It requires acts that can only be described as "moste evile") or how to gain covert access to titles in the Restricted Section, you don't need a vial of Felix Felicis in your pocket to know you're in luck.

Chockablock with potions, textbooks, professors, classroom descriptions, exam schedules and more, this handy guide is your authority on all the known subjects covered at Britain's most famous school for wizards. Featuring Muggle-adjacent trivia that would astonish even a seasoned expert like Arthur Weasley, it's sure to illuminate the ins and outs of a Hogwarts education faster than you can learn to cast the Wand-Lighting Charm. Keep your wand at the ready and read on to discover all there is to learn at the school that made Harry Potter a hero.

---

*Professor Flitwick would stress that you should by no means summon an untold number of salamanders to come flying at you.

Table of Contents

A Note From MuggleNet

As the number one resource for all things *Harry Potter*, MuggleNet has dedicated nearly a quarter of a century to analyzing all things relating to the Boy Who Lived. By magical means that clearly defy Gamp's Law of Elemental Transfiguration, J.K. Rowling's best-selling series conjured blockbuster films, a successful Broadway play, world-class theme parks and more, all of which hinge on wizards coming into their power. That's where Hogwarts School of Witchcraft and Wizardry comes in.

If Rubeus Hagrid had been able to provide 11-year-old Harry a glimpse of just how much his life would change by attending Britain's most famous magical school, it's possible Harry would've run screaming out of the hut on the rock and plummeted into the sea (or, you know, flown onto the roof, but that's beside the point). Fortunately for us readers, Hagrid keeps it limited to "Yer a wizard" over birthday cake, and we get to watch Hogwarts mold the lonely adolescent into a capable, confident member of the magical community deft at dueling and Defense Against the Dark Arts.

These hallowed halls aren't just the place where Harry makes lifelong friends, falls in love and grows closer to the parents he never knew, though—Hogwarts is also where he learns to de-escalate conflict, temper his anger, stand up for himself and help others do the same. It's no wonder Voldemort brings the fight to Harry's doorstep at the one place the Boy Who Lived feels safe. Naturally, the only way Harry makes it through this battle is by calling on the knowledge instilled in him by a number of brilliant professors, skills that have been passed down through generations.

Those of us who've wanted to linger on the ramparts of the Astronomy Tower, gaze upon the odd and dusty ingredients secreted away in Snape's Potions storeroom or face our greatest fears by turning them into something hilarious know just how alluring the charms and dangers of Hogwarts can be. Until we can each take our place under the Sorting Hat, this book is the next best thing when it comes to discovering all that goes into receiving a magical education.

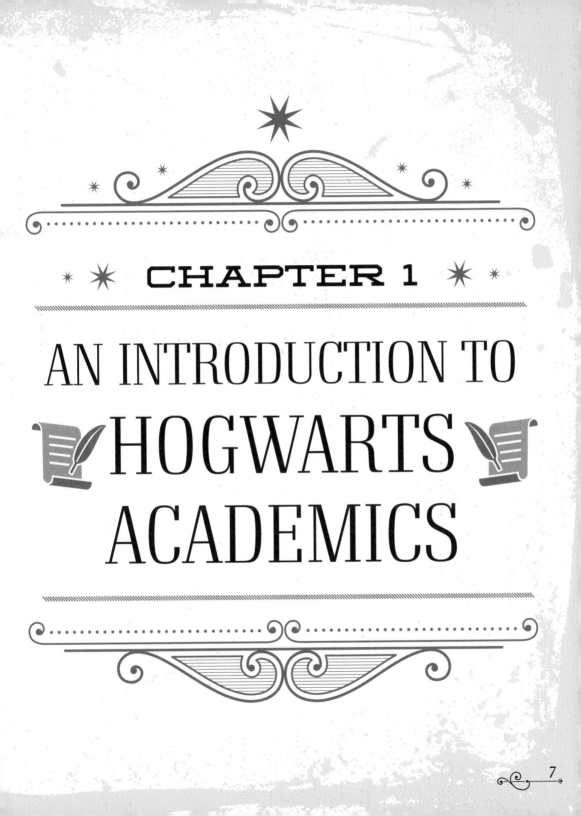

CHAPTER 1

AN INTRODUCTION TO HOGWARTS ACADEMICS

Sorting Ceremony

The Sorting Ceremony is one of the most pivotal events Hogwarts students experience during their seven years at the school. Before gorging themselves at the start-of-term feast, they are Sorted into one of the four Houses by the Sorting Hat, once the chapeau of Godric Gryffindor but now charmed to allow the Sorting of students to continue after the Hogwarts founders died. Every year, the hat sings a new song of its own composition before the ceremony begins. The song usually makes note of the traits that represent each House, though during Harry's fifth year, it also hints at the difficult times ahead. Harry only hears the Sorting Hat's song during his first, fourth and fifth years.

Sorting creates a sense of camaraderie and belonging, which helps students like Harry, who is new to the magical community, settle into their new home. It also allows students to learn something about themselves that they might not have recognized prior to the ceremony. In 1991, Neville Longbottom pleads with the Sorting Hat to be placed in Hufflepuff, sure he will be unable to live up to the reputation that comes with being a Gryffindor, but the Sorting Hat Sorts him into Gryffindor anyway. While Neville didn't understand why at the time, he likely did later following his courageous efforts during Voldemort's downfall.

Because each House is known for certain characteristics, some Houses are believed to only produce a certain type of witch or wizard. It's commonly thought that Slytherin only produces Dark wizards, though it isn't the only House from which Dark wizards emerge. The House system causes students to forget that some of all the House qualities are in everyone and that House members aren't limited to a handful of personality traits; ultimately, the system can foster prejudice and discrimination.

House Points System

Every student can earn and lose points for their House throughout the school year for the chance to win the House Cup. The points earned in House Quidditch matches also contribute to the House Cup. Students can see how many points their House has by viewing the hourglasses in the entrance hall. Each hourglass is filled with gems that correspond with the colors of each House: rubies for Gryffindor, diamonds for Hufflepuff, sapphires for Ravenclaw and emeralds for Slytherin.

Students have several opportunities to earn House points by correctly answering questions in class, receiving a perfect grade on a quiz, helping other students in sticky situations and performing great deeds (e.g., saving a student from a secret chamber in the school). The points earned in House Quidditch matches also contribute to winning the Cup, and students can be awarded House points for events that take place off Hogwarts grounds, as Harry and his friends discover after fighting off Death Eaters at the Ministry of Magic during Harry's fifth year.

Of course, House points can be lost for common infractions, such as tardiness, interrupting lessons, being out after curfew or talking back to a professor. Other situations, like pretending to be Dementors during a Quidditch match or throwing animal hearts at other students, have also resulted in lost House points. Sometimes points are deducted unfairly by teachers abusing their power. Snape, for example, is not above deducting points for a student being a "know-it-all." Professors have the authority to award and deduct points, as do prefects during Harry's second year. By Harry's fifth year, however, this rule appears to have been modified since prefects cannot deduct points, though members of Umbridge's Inquisitorial Squad can. This results in points taken from Gryffindor for absurd reasons, such as contradicting a squad member or having an untucked shirt.

Detention and Punishment Systems

DETENTION

A common punishment, detentions have been given for wandering the castle after curfew, crashing a car into the Whomping Willow, criticizing teachers and melting cauldrons.

Detentions take many forms during Harry's time at Hogwarts: As a first year, Harry completes detention in the Forbidden Forest with Hagrid, whereas in his second year, he is forced to help Professor Lockhart answer fan mail.

EXPULSION

Although frequently threatened, expulsion is rarely employed—and only as a last resort. When a student is expelled, their wand is snapped in half, an act signifying they will be unable to become true members of wizarding society. Newt Scamander and Rubeus Hagrid are two students known to have been expelled. Hagrid's wand was broken when he was accused of opening the Chamber of Secrets, but even though he was accused of endangering students with a magical creature, Scamander's was not.

CRUEL AND UNUSUAL PUNISHMENT

Umbridge's presence at Hogwarts ushers in an era of extremism. The enactment of educational decrees from the Ministry of Magic gives her the authority to decide all punishments. In detentions, Umbridge employs a quill of her own invention that etches the words a student writes into the back of their hand, using their blood as ink.

During the 1997–1998 school year, Alecto and Amycus Carrow require students to perform the Cruciatus Curse on those given detention. Some students are kept in chains. Those who try to protect others are tortured.

Umbridge's Decrees

During the 1995–1996 school year, the Ministry of Magic enacts a series of eight new educational decrees to limit Albus Dumbledore's power at Hogwarts. This brings the total number of educational decrees to 29, though the first 21 are unknown.

Educational Decree Number 22, enacted on August 30, 1995, states that "in the event of the current headmaster being unable to provide a candidate for a teaching post, the Ministry should select an appropriate person." This is the means by which Umbridge becomes a professor. In September, Educational Decree Number 23 installs Umbridge as High Inquisitor, a position that gives her the authority to review the lessons of other professors, put them on probation and even remove them from their posts.

After Harry's meeting at the Hog's Head, the Ministry passes Educational Decree Number 24, requiring the High Inquisitor's approval for all student-run activities and clubs. Educational Decree Number 25 gives Umbridge "supreme authority over all punishments." This decree is conveniently revealed following the Gryffindor vs. Slytherin Quidditch match, allowing her to ban Harry, Fred and George from playing.

The decrees continue with Number 26, barring teachers from sharing any information outside of their course subjects with students. Educational Decree Number 27, enacted after Harry's interview on Voldemort's return is published in *The Quibbler,* states that "any student found in possession of the magazine *The Quibbler* will be expelled."

After Dumbledore's Army is discovered and the headmaster takes the blame, Educational Decrees Number 28 and 29 are declared, making Umbridge the headmistress and permitting Filch to use barbaric corporal punishment. The decrees are done away with after Dumbledore is reinstated as Hogwarts's headmaster following the sighting of Voldemort at the Ministry.

Recreational Activities for Professors

There are myriad ways professors can relax when they aren't teaching students or attending to their other duties. Several professors, including Remus Lupin and Rubeus Hagrid, enjoy having tea with students in their spare time.

Many of the professors watch the school's Quidditch matches, cheering on their Houses and acting as authority figures or referees when necessary. Professor Lockart had been enjoying the 1992–1993 Gryffindor vs. Slytherin match when he eagerly "fixed" Harry's broken arm, while Professor Quirrell had more sinister plans at the same event the previous year.

In terms of less violent downtime activities, Professor Quirrell enjoys pressing flowers, a hobby he likely acquired during his international travels. Professor McGonagall corrects articles in *Transfiguration Today* and does needlework. Ever the extrovert, Professor Slughorn hosts club meetings and parties for his invite-only Slug Club in addition to collecting rare and valuable items like Acromantula venom.

When not in their office or classroom, professors can retreat to the staffroom, which includes a wardrobe for professors' robes. They can also take a load off in one of several mismatched chairs. Professor Binns, the History of Magic professor, likely enjoyed spending his free time taking naps in front of the fire in the staffroom, which is where his colleagues found him after he passed away.

Like anyone else, professors have to shop and take care of personal business, so it's not uncommon to see a professor in Hogsmeade on the weekends or Diagon Alley prior to the beginning of the term. While trying to get to Diagon Alley just before his second year, Harry runs into Hagrid in Knockturn Alley while the half-giant is busy purchasing Flesh-Eating Slug repellent for his garden.

Menus and Food Offerings at Hogwarts

Meals at Hogwarts are served in the Great Hall. House-elves in the kitchens prepare meals, which are magically sent to the tables above. Standard school fare includes Cornish pasties, roast beef, stew and Yorkshire pudding. Special dishes are known to appear on the menu for different occasions. Notably, when Beauxbatons students arrive at the beginning of the 1994–1995 school year to take part in the Triwizard Tournament festivities, bouillabaisse is made available. During the holidays, Christmas cake and eggnog make a welcome appearance.

KNOWN FOODS AT HOGWARTS:

- Apple Pie
- Bacon and Steak
- Baked Pumpkin
- Beef Casserole
- Black Pudding
- Boiled Potatoes
- Chipolatas
- Chips (Fries)
- Chocolate Éclairs
- Chocolate Gateau
- Christmas Cake
- Christmas Pudding
- Cornish Pasties
- Cranberry Sauce
- Crumpets
- Eggnog
- Eggs
- Fried Tomatoes
- Gravy
- Ham Sandwiches
- Jam Doughnuts
- Lamb Chops
- Mashed Potatoes
- Peppermint Humbugs
- Pork Chops
- Rice Pudding
- Roast Beef
- Roast Chicken
- Sausage
- Shepherd's Pie
- Spotted Dick
- Sprouts
- Steak
- Steak & Kidney Pudding
- Stew
- Treacle Tart
- Trifle
- Tripe
- Turkey
- Yorkshire Pudding

Classes by Year

First-year Hogwarts students are required to take a set of core classes to kickstart their magical education. Students continue with this core coursework until after taking their O.W.L. examinations in their fifth year. Upon reaching their sixth year of study, students are given the option to drop a core class if it doesn't align with their future goals or if they failed to achieve a high enough O.W.L. score to continue with the subject.

YEARS 1 AND 2

Astronomy classes at Hogwarts align with the Muggle version of studying the night sky. Students learn the names of stars, track the movement of planets and complete detailed star charts.

Charms is an essential subject for witches and wizards. From Summoning Charms to levitating objects, the subject provides a base of spellwork that proves useful in a variety of settings.

Defense Against the Dark Arts prepares students to protect themselves against Dark magic. Lessons include how to cast defensive spells and how to recognize dangerous creatures and cursed objects.

> **Note:** Dark Arts becomes a core class during the 1997–1998 school year after the fall of the Ministry of Magic and the subsequent Death Eater control of Hogwarts.

Flying is a required course for first-year students, but it is not known to be offered beyond that level. First years learn how to summon their broomsticks and properly guide them through the sky.

Herbology is the wizarding equivalent of botany. The class teaches students how to identify, care for and use magical plants.

History of Magic covers significant past events of the magical community. Some known lesson subjects include goblin rebellions, giant wars and the International Warlock Conventions of 1289 and 1709.

Potions consists of learning to brew magical draughts and potions from various ingredients.

Transfiguration familiarizes students with the art of transforming the appearance of an object or a living thing. The subject is considered both complex and dangerous.

YEARS 3 THROUGH 7

Upon entering their third year at Hogwarts, students are required to choose two electives. Students may choose more than two, but scheduling may prove challenging. During the 1993 school year, Hermione Granger takes all five electives with the help of a Time-Turner. Additional electives may be offered in students' sixth and seventh years.

Alchemy classes may be offered to sixth-year students when there is sufficient demand. Alchemy involves the study of the four basic elements: air, earth, fire, and water, which students learn to manipulate for the purpose of transforming one substance into another.

Ancient Runes are a form of writing used by witches and wizards long ago. Coursework involves translating the meaning of runes to modern English.

Apparition is a 12-week course that costs 12 Galleons. Only offered to students who are 17 or will be turning 17 by the end of that August, the class covers how to disappear from one location and reappear in another.

Arithmancy teaches students the magical properties of numbers.

Care of Magical Creatures is the wizarding equivalent of zoology or animal sciences.

Divination teaches students to predict the future using such methods as consulting crystal balls, reading tea leaves, deciphering visions and stargazing.

Muggle Studies examines the history and day-to-day lives of non-magical people. Though typically an elective, the course is made mandatory for all students in 1997 when Death Eater Alecto Carrow takes over the subject. As a follower of Voldemort, Carrow presents a slanted view of Muggles.

Textbooks

Each year, prior to the start of term, Hogwarts students are provided with a list of required texts. Professors assign books based on their lesson plans for the year. Due to the high turnover in the position of Defense Against the Dark Arts teacher, the required textbooks for that particular class tend to vary from year to year.

Students can find all the supplies on their lists in Diagon Alley, including their assigned reading. The bookseller, Flourish and Blotts, keeps its shelves stocked with the texts assigned by Hogwarts professors.

In 1992, the bookstore sells copies of Gilderoy Lockhart titles and even hosts a book signing event with the author/adventurer while students and their families are shopping for back-to-school supplies. Having just acquired the job of Defense Against the Dark Arts professor, Lockhart assigns the entirety of his published works to his students.

The following year, the shop carries copies of *The Monster Book of Monsters*, which is assigned by newly appointed Care of Magical Creatures professor Rubeus Hagrid. Much to the manager's chagrin, the copies keep attacking each other (an incident he claims is worse than when the entire stock of *The Invisible Book of Invisibility* disappeared), prompting him to vow to never carry the book again.

While new titles crop up from year to year as staff change and lesson plans are altered, there is one mainstay on Hogwarts reading lists: Miranda Goshawk's *Standard Book of Spells* series. The author wrote a volume for each of the seven grade levels at Hogwarts. *A History of Magic* by Bathilda Bagshot is also required reading for students for all seven years of their Hogwarts schooling.

Sample Class Schedule

HARRY POTTER'S FOURTH-YEAR* CLASS SCHEDULE (1994-1995)

MONDAY	TUESDAY	WEDNESDAY	THURSDAY	FRIDAY
Herbology with *Hufflepuff***	History of Magic		Transfiguration	History of Magic
BREAK	*BREAK*	*BREAK*	*BREAK*	*BREAK*
Care of Magical Creatures with *Slytherin*		Charms		Charms
LUNCH	*LUNCH*	*LUNCH*	*LUNCH*	*LUNCH*
Divination	Potions		Defense Against the Dark Arts	Potions with *Slytherin*
Divination			Defense Against the Dark Arts	Potions with *Slytherin*
DINNER	*DINNER*	*DINNER*	*DINNER*	*DINNER*

*Gray boxes in the schedule represent undocumented periods of time. Astronomy is not mentioned during Harry's fourth year, but it likely takes place after dinner on Tuesday, Wednesday or Thursday.
**Students from two Houses will occasionally share a class, but for the most part, classes are composed of students from the same House.

Exams

Hogwarts students are required to test their knowledge of various subjects. Here's what we know about exams based on Harry's time at the school.

1991–1992 SCHOOL YEAR
First week of June
- **Charms** Make a pineapple tap-dance across a desk
- **History of Magic** Wizard who invented self-stirring cauldrons
- **Potions** Forgetfulness Potion
- **Transfiguration** Turn a mouse into a snuff box

1992–1993 SCHOOL YEAR
End-of-year exams are canceled.

1993–1994 SCHOOL YEAR
Beginning of June
- **Care of Magical Creatures** Keep a Flobberworm alive for one hour
- **Charms** Cheering Charms
- **Defense Against the Dark Arts** Traverse an obstacle course containing a grindylow, a hinkypunk, a boggart and red caps

- **Divination** Read a crystal ball
- **History of Magic** Describe medieval witch hunts
- **Potions** Confusing Concoction
- **Transfiguration** Turn a teapot into a tortoise

1994–1995 SCHOOL YEAR
Mid-June
- **History of Magic** List rebels involved in the goblin rebellions

1995–1996 SCHOOL YEAR
During their fifth year, students take O.W.L. exams (see page opposite) rather than the usual end-of-term tests

1996–1997 SCHOOL YEAR
Late June
All end-of-year exams are postponed due to Dumbledore's death

O.W.L.s

Ordinary Wizarding Levels—otherwise known as O.W.L.s—are subject-specific exams taken by Hogwarts students at the end of their fifth year at the school. These standardized tests are administered by the Wizarding Examinations Authority and are often divided into two portions: theoretical (written) and practical (demonstration). O.W.L. scores largely determine the trajectory of a student's future, including if a student will be allowed to continue studying a subject during their remaining time at Hogwarts and even what career opportunities are available for them upon graduation. If a student receives any passing grade on a subject's O.W.L. exam, it is colloquially known as "getting an O.W.L."

PASSING GRADES:
- Outstanding
- Exceeds Expectations
- Acceptable

FAILING GRADES:
- Poor
- Dreadful
- Troll

ADVANCED COURSEWORK

Professors at Hogwarts use O.W.L. scores to determine which students are prepared to continue studying certain subjects at an advanced level. Requirements for these tests are set by individual professors, meaning that a change in staff could result in a higher or lower standard.

CAREER CHOICES

Many careers in the magical community require a certain set of N.E.W.T. scores (see pg. 25) to begin training. To be admitted into N.E.W.T.-level classes at Hogwarts, students must successfully obtain satisfactory scores on their O.W.L.s. Near the end of their fifth year, Hogwarts students are given pamphlets advertising different career path options;

these pamphlets outline the necessary academic background required to be considered qualified.

AUROR WITH THE MINISTRY OF MAGIC

Required Scores Five N.E.W.T.s scored at Exceeds Expectations or higher

Note It is unclear if the Ministry of Magic prefers certain subjects or if any five are acceptable so long as the required N.E.W.T. score is obtained. During Harry's fifth year, McGonagall suggests that if he wishes to become an Auror, he should consider Charms, Defense Against the Dark Arts, Potions and Transfiguration.

CURSE BREAKER AT GRINGOTTS WIZARDING BANK

Required Scores An unknown Arithmancy score

Note The position is described as a challenging and thrilling one that involves "travel, adventure, and substantial danger-related treasure bonuses." It is extremely likely that advanced N.E.W.T. scores in Charms, Defense Against the Dark Arts, Potions and Transfiguration are required. Ancient Runes may also be encouraged.

KNOWN REQUIREMENTS TO ADVANCE TO N.E.W.T.-LEVEL COURSES

CHARMS
• **Filius Flitwick**
Acceptable (possible) or
Exceeds Expectations (likely)*

POTIONS
• **Severus Snape**
Outstanding
• **Horace Slughorn**
Exceeds Expectations

TRANSFIGURATION
• **Minerva McGonagall**
Exceeds Expectations

BANNED ITEMS

Anti-cheating spells are applied to exam papers, and the following items are banned: Auto-Answer Quills, Detachable Cribbing Cuffs, Remembralls and Self-Correcting Ink.

*When Harry expresses his desire to become an Auror, McGonagall explains how his Charms scores have been between Acceptable and Exceeds Expectations, deeming it "satisfactory." Considering the Ministry requires five N.E.W.T.s scored at an Exceeds Expectations or above, it can be deduced that Professor Flitwick requires an Exceeds Expectations O.W.L. to continue with Charms in the sixth year.

HEALER AT ST. MUNGO'S HOSPITAL
FOR MAGICAL MALADIES AND INJURIES
Required Scores A minimum score of Exceeds Expectations at N.E.W.T.
level in Charms, Defense Against the Dark Arts, Herbology, Potions and
Transfiguration.

MUGGLE RELATIONS (PRESUMABLY AT THE
MINISTRY OF MAGIC)
Required Scores An O.W.L. in Muggle Studies
Note Candidates are encouraged to consider a career in Muggle
relations if they value enthusiasm, patience and "a good sense of fun."

EXAM SCHEDULE

O.W.L.s take place over two weeks at the end of the school year. A
student's course load determines how many exams for different subjects
they have on a given day. Students who have opted to take more electives
(e.g., Hermione) may receive fewer breaks than students who take fewer
electives (e.g., Harry and Ron). Most exams are split into two portions, with
a theoretical (written) portion given in the morning and, after students
break for lunch, a practical (demonstration) portion given in the afternoon.

1995–1996 O.W.L. SCHEDULE

WEEK 1
MONDAY MORNING
Charms *Theoretical*
This exam is administered in the
Great Hall. The four House tables
are replaced with rows of individual
tables facing the staff table, where
the exam's proctor(s) stands
alongside a large hourglass,
spare quills, ink bottles and rolls
of parchment.
Known Content Cheering Charms,
the incantation and wand movement
required to make objects fly
Known Proctors Professor
McGonagall

MONDAY AFTERNOON
Charms *Practical*
Students are gathered in a small room adjacent to the Great Hall where they wait their turn to be called in alphabetical order. Inside the Great Hall, proctors have positioned themselves a distance away from one another, and students are directed to whichever proctor is free.
Known Content Make an eggcup do cartwheels, perform Levitation and Color Change Charms
Known Proctors Professor Marchbanks and Professor Tofty (Wizarding Examinations Authority)

TUESDAY MORNING
Transfiguration *Theoretical*
Known Content The definition of a Switching Spell

TUESDAY AFTERNOON
Transfiguration *Practical*
Known Content Vanish an iguana or ferret

WEDNESDAY AFTERNOON
Herbology *Practical*
Known Content Handle a Fanged Geranium

THURSDAY MORNING
Defense Against the Dark Arts *Theoretical*

THURSDAY AFTERNOON
Defense Against the Dark Arts *Practical*
Known Content Perform counterjinxes and defensive spells, Boggart Banishing Spell
Note: Professor Tofty asks Harry to produce a Patronus for a bonus point
Known Proctors Professor Tofty (Wizarding Examinations Authority)

FRIDAY
Ancient Runes *Theoretical**
Known Content Translate *ehwaz*

WEEK 2
MONDAY MORNING
Potions *Theoretical*
Known Content Describe the effects of Polyjuice Potion

MONDAY AFTERNOON
Potions *Practical*
Known Content Brew an unknown potion and collect a sample
Known Proctors Professor Marchbanks (Wizarding Examinations Authority)

TUESDAY AFTERNOON
Care of Magical Creatures
Practical
This exam takes place on the lawn on the edge of the Forbidden Forest, near Hagrid's hut.
Known Content Identify a Knarl from a hedgehog, correctly handle a Bowtruckle, feed and clean a Fire Crab without being burned, correctly identify the diet that should be given to a sick unicorn
Known Proctors
Unknown witch (Wizarding Examinations Authority)

WEDNESDAY MORNING
Astronomy *Theoretical*
Known Content Name all of Jupiter's moons

WEDNESDAY AFTERNOON
Arithmancy
Divination *Practical*

Known Content Read a crystal ball, read tea leaves, read a palm

WEDNESDAY NIGHT
Astronomy *Practical*
Known Content Fill in a star chart with the current positions of stars and planets
Known Proctors Professor Marchbanks and Professor Tofty (Wizarding Examinations Authority)

THURSDAY AFTERNOON
History of Magic *Theoretical**
Known Content Wand legislation's effect on goblin riots of the 18th century, the 1749 breach of the Statute of Secrecy, the formation of the International Confederation of Wizards
Known Proctors Professor Marchbanks and Professor Tofty (Wizarding Examinations Authority)

---

*It is highly unlikely that Ancient Runes or History of Magic have a practical portion of the examination due to the nature of the subjects.

KNOWN O.W.L.s RECEIVED BY HOGWARTS STUDENTS (BY SUBJECT)

- **Ancient Runes** Hermione Granger, Bill Weasley, Percy Weasley
- **Arithmancy** Hermione Granger, Bill Weasley, Percy Weasley
- **Astronomy** Hermione Granger, Harry Potter, Bill Weasley, Percy Weasley, Ron Weasley
- **Care of Magical Creatures** Hermione Granger, Angelina Johnson, Harry Potter, Bill Weasley, Percy Weasley, Ron Weasley
- **Charms** Lavender Brown, Cedric Diggory, Seamus Finnigan, Hermione Granger, Neville Longbottom, Harry Potter, Alicia Spinnet, Dean Thomas, Bill Weasley, Fred Weasley, George Weasley, Percy Weasley, Ron Weasley
- **Defense Against the Dark Arts** Lavender Brown, Seamus Finnigan, Hermione Granger, Lee Jordan, Neville Longbottom, Ernie Macmillan, Draco Malfoy, Pansy Parkinson, Parvati Patil, Harry Potter, Dean Thomas, Bill Weasley, Fred Weasley, George Weasley, Percy Weasley, Ron Weasley
- **Divination** Parvati Patil, Bill Weasley, Percy Weasley
- **Herbology** Hannah Abbott, Hermione Granger, Neville Longbottom, Harry Potter, Bill Weasley, Fred Weasley, George Weasley, Percy Weasley, Ron Weasley
- **History of Magic** Hermione Granger, Bill Weasley, Percy Weasley
- **Muggle Studies** Bill Weasley, Percy Weasley
- **Potions** Terry Boot, Michael Corner, Hermione Granger, Ernie Macmillan, Draco Malfoy, Theodore Nott, Harry Potter, Bill Weasley, Percy Weasley, Ron Weasley, Blaise Zabini
- **Transfiguration** Katie Bell, Lavender Brown, Cedric Diggory, Seamus Finnigan, Hermione Granger, Neville Longbottom, Draco Malfoy, Parvati Patil, Harry Potter, Dean Thomas, Bill Weasley, Percy Weasley, Ron Weasley

DID YOU KNOW?

During Harry's practical Astronomy O.W.L. exam, he and his peers are distracted from the test by the assault on Hagrid and McGonagall by Umbridge, which they can clearly see from their position in the Astronomy Tower.

N.E.W.T.s

The Nastily Exhausting Wizarding Test (N.E.W.T.) is the highest level of standardized examination taken by Hogwarts students. Once students complete their O.W.L.s (see pg. 19) in their fifth year, they become N.E.W.T. students for their sixth and seventh years. N.E.W.T.s are generally regarded as important; these grades affect which careers students may or may not be able to pursue as well as whether or not they may advance to further specialized training upon finishing their schooling.

Most students tend to be selective regarding which courses to continue for their N.E.W.T.s, choosing to take only those subjects in which they excel and/or those that would serve them in their chosen career path. The grades students earn for their O.W.L.s determine which classes they can take at the N.E.W.T. level. In their fifth year, each student meets individually with their head of House for career advice to assist in preparation for O.W.L.s and to ensure the student's goals for their last two school years align with their aspirations beyond school. For example, prospective Aurors are required to secure five N.E.W.T.s and nothing below the grade of Exceeds Expectations. Furthermore, each professor has a set O.W.L. grade they require for students to advance to N.E.W.T. level. Professor Snape, for example, only accepts students who earn an Outstanding on their O.W.L. into N.E.W.T.-level Potions. A student whose grade is lacking would be advised to put in more effort leading up to their O.W.L. to make it to N.E.W.T. level.

Requirements can, however, vary in accordance with staff changes; when Professor Slughorn returns to his role of Potions Master in 1996, sixth-year students who had achieved an E in their Potions O.W.L. were accepted into his class. These factors can be a cause of great distress in students who have not achieved the requisite grade on their O.W.L.s for their own aspirations or as desired by parents or guardians. While some students agonize over their N.E.W.T. and career prospects, others take on a more indifferent mindset. Some students hoping to pursue less traditional paths opt to leave school early with only their O.W.L.s, although they do have the option to return to Hogwarts to complete their N.E.W.T.s.

At the start of term in sixth year, the head of House visits each student to discuss and distribute class schedules. Students must confer with the professor and confirm which subjects to take and which to drop. Career aspirations, O.W.L. grades and each teacher's own requirements must be considered. The head of House taps each schedule with his or her wand to make final adjustments before handing it to the student. Because N.E.W.T. students limit their focus of studies, many students are delighted to find they have several break periods between classes in their sixth year. Their delight is often short-lived: Once these students begin their advanced learning, they discover these break times must be dedicated to rigorous study and, as it turns out, nastily exhausting coursework.

While younger students often attend their classes with all their fellow students within their own House and perhaps one other House, N.E.W.T. students may take a class with students from all four Houses due to the limited number of pupils taking each subject. Some professors may find they have very few (and in some cases no) students who choose to continue their subject at N.E.W.T. level.

Coursework for N.E.W.T. students is incredibly advanced. For example, Conjuring Spells, which are known to be more difficult compared to Vanishing Spells, are only taught in N.E.W.T.-level Transfiguration, and the Protean Charm is understood to be N.E.W.T. standard. Meanwhile, Thestrals are more likely to be introduced in sixth-year Care of Magical Creatures, and students study complicated brews like Amortentia, Felix Felicis, Polyjuice Potion and Veritaserum in N.E.W.T.-level Potions. These brews are highly difficult to make, contributing to their placement in this capstone curriculum. It should be noted that abusing any of these dangerous potions has serious repercussions. In some instances, law-breaking witches and wizards might even be legally prosecuted.

Teaching Philosophies

There are as many different teaching philosophies at Hogwarts as there are professors, as evidenced through chosen texts and content, the structure of assignments and assessments, and interactions with students. Throughout Harry's time at the school, magic is presented as fixed and precise yet simultaneously enigmatic and chaotic. While coursework tends to skew toward the former theory of magic, circumstances generally reveal the truth of the latter.

When it comes to the myriad approaches for informing students' magical educations, one of the main differences comes down to the distinction between theory-based learning and more hands-on, practical experiences. First-year students might be eager to start casting spells at the start of term, but professors generally adopt scaffolding methods, beginning with basic lecturing before asking students to attempt the most rudimentary magic. In later years, it is not uncommon for practical learning to take place on the first day of classes. Professors such as Cuthbert Binns and Dolores Umbridge dedicate all classes to reading and note-taking, while Rubeus Hagrid, Remus Lupin and Barty Crouch, Jr. (while impersonating Alastor Moody), prefer a learn-by-doing methodology. Students tend to favor the practical approach where they engage in activities such as using their wands and other equipment, solving problems and interacting with peers and creatures. Such experiences prepare students for practical examinations, the Triwizard Tournament and real-life scenarios outside of school. Still, students often require a strong basis of theoretical knowledge in order to properly master certain skills or spells. For example, Severus Snape does not offer Harry a detailed explanation of how Occlumency works, a choice that ultimately results in Harry's failure to master the skill (of course, the shared enmity between the two doesn't help).

Professors select textbooks and decide what content will be studied at each level in accordance with their philosophy and style. For example, Umbridge, who wants risk-free study of the theoretical tenets of defensive magic, selects *Defensive Magical Theory*, a text that does not provide information about using defensive spells. Hagrid, who sees fun and excitement in the most off-putting creatures, assigns an especially monstrous book that students are afraid to open: *The Monster Book of Monsters*. Gilderoy Lockhart, on the other hand, cares more about adoration than his students' education and takes the opportunity to assign his own published works as required reading.

Some professors, such as Binns, make no effort to get to know their students. Others, like Snape and Slughorn, exhibit strong favoritism. These practices do not always command respect or establish a connection with pupils who are not in their favor. Snape goes as far as to exact cruelty on students by expecting perfection, erasing dissatisfactory work and publicly shaming students. Umbridge is similar but goes even further. Such individuals are, however, the exception rather than the rule: Many teachers are kind and encouraging and have a vested interest in their students' success. Lupin, for example, cultivates a strong rapport with students by acknowledging each of them by name during their first class.

RAMIFICATIONS OF THE ABSENCE OF MUGGLE SUBJECTS

Before their 11th birthday, witches and wizards are taught by their parents or attend a non-magical school. Presumably, students arrive at Hogwarts with at least the ability to read and write, but their other educational milestones may vary.

There is some crossover between Hogwarts subjects and Muggle subjects, including Astronomy, History, Potions (chemistry), Herbology (botany), Flying (physical education), Apparition (driver's education) and Muggle Studies (anthropology/sociology). Still, this intersection is limited, and there are likely ramifications for the absence of other course offerings. While mathematics is touched on in Arithmancy and likely studied by prospective Gringotts workers, it is unclear if students understand algebra or geometry. Hogwarts students may not be well versed in historical and current events outside of the magical community.

Other topics offered in Muggle schools are entirely absent. For example, without language arts, students may struggle to improve their writing skills for essays. In fact, without studying literature, students may lack communication skills, critical thinking, empathy and ethics (as most notably evidenced by Rita Skeeter). An absence of art, theater and creative writing classes leaves little room for self-expression. Hogwarts students also go without formal education on geography, foreign languages, home economics and childcare. The lack of physics may be forgiven, since magic often supersedes this branch of science.

Perhaps the most critical deficiency at Hogwarts is in health and wellness offerings. Physical education is limited to first-year Flying lessons and those who make the Quidditch team, and Hogwarts students must go through puberty without instruction. Given the dangers of attending a school with magical accidents and yearly attacks, one would expect a school counselor to be made available. So many parts of the human experience are difficult to navigate without guidance. For a student who suffers immeasurable trauma like Harry, regular sessions with a trained counselor would be more beneficial than the limited capacity of his head of House.

ANECDOTES, TIPS AND WARNINGS

From cautioning students to be mindful of their spellwork to sharing funny stories of their experiences, Hogwarts teachers are anything but boring. During Harry's first year, Professor Flitwick recounts a tale to ensure students remember to take caution, particularly while mastering the Levitation Charm. "Never forget Wizard Baruffio, who said 's' instead of 'f' and found himself on the floor with a buffalo on his chest."

Tutoring

Extra practice is what makes good students better, and a few Hogwarts professors lend their expertise to students after hours.

PROFESSOR REMUS LUPIN
SUBJECT: Defense Against the Dark Arts
In 1994, Lupin tutors Harry after hours to help him master the Patronus Charm to defend himself against Dementors that have been sent to Hogwarts following Sirius Black's escape from Azkaban. To immediately put his homework into practice, Lupin has Harry perform the spell on a boggart.

PROFESSOR SEVERUS SNAPE
SUBJECT: Occlumency
During the 1995-1996 academic year, Dumbledore tasks Snape, a skilled Occlumens, with instructing Harry in the art of closing off one's mind to unwelcome intruders in an attempt to keep him safe from Lord Voldemort. Snape trains Harry by invading his mind and having Harry attempt to block it with mixed results. For more on Occlumency, see pg. 186.

PROFESSOR ALBUS DUMBLEDORE
SUBJECT: Voldemort/Horcruxes
During the 1996–1997 school year, Professor Dumbledore gives Harry special lessons that focus on Voldemort's past. He uses a Pensieve to show Harry various people's memories of Voldemort's early life, eventually confirming the theory that Voldemort has created several Horcruxes that Harry needs to destroy.

STUDENTS WHO TUTORED EACH OTHER

During Harry's fourth year at Hogwarts, Hermione helps Harry master the Summoning Charm. The following school year, when Defense Against the Dark Arts professor Dolores Umbridge prohibits students from practicing spellwork, Harry leads after-class lessons in performing defensive spells in the Room of Requirement as the leader of Dumbledore's Army.

THE CLASSES THAT HELP THE TRIO THE MOST

Of the various subjects Harry, Ron and Hermione take at Hogwarts, a few prove particularly useful.

Charms

Ever a quick study, Hermione employs various charms while the trio hunts Horcruxes to ensure they stay hidden from Voldemort and his Death Eaters.

Defense Against the Dark Arts

This is arguably the most useful subject to Harry and his friends throughout their time at Hogwarts as well as in their battle against Voldemort. The spells and skills covered in this subject assist Harry during the Triwizard Tournament and help the trio and their friends stand their ground against Death Eaters during the Battle of the Department of Mysteries, the hunt for Horcruxes and the Battle of Hogwarts.

Potions

Hermione uses the skills she has learned in Potions class to brew Polyjuice Potion in the trio's second year in an attempt to invade the Slytherin common room to find out whether or not Draco Malfoy is the Heir of Slytherin.

Teachers' Contributions

Despite busy schedules, Hogwarts's talented teachers often go the extra mile for the school and their students. Whether that means helping host the Triwizard Tournament or assisting headmaster Albus Dumbledore with hiding a powerful object, they're ready to lend their skills and expertise whenever the need arises.

Hogwarts professors might be very academically focused, but they also occasionally take the time to make the environment more fun and magical. Every year, Hagrid accompanies the first-year students as they journey to the school via boat across the lake. He also provides the school with 12 Christmas trees, which Professor Flitwick usually decorates, sometimes with the help of Professor McGonagall.

While the staff surely knows how to have fun, they're also incredibly skilled—during the 1991–1992 academic year, each does their best to keep Voldemort from acquiring the Sorcerer's Stone. The professors work together by creating a challenging, intricate obstacle course. Hagrid provides Fluffy, the vicious three-headed dog, to guard the trapdoor; Sprout installs Devil's Snare to entangle any intruders; Flitwick enchants hundreds of flying keys, of which only one can unlock a door to the next challenge; McGonagall creates a gigantic wizard chess set requiring any would-be Stone snatcher to win the game. Professor Quirrell provides a troll, while Professor Snape contributes several potions (of which three are poisonous) along with a riddle that requires logic to solve. Finally, Dumbledore lends the finishing touch to the obstacle course with the last hurdle: the Mirror of Erised, where he hides the Stone, which can only be acquired by someone who seeks to have but not use the object.

The following school year, when a basilisk wreaks havoc by Petrifying people, two teachers combine their talents to save the victims: Professor Sprout grows mandrakes, and Snape uses them to brew a potion that wakes the affected individuals.

When Remus Lupin takes the job of teaching Defense Against the Dark Arts in 1993, Snape (reluctantly) brews the Wolfsbane Potion to help the lycanthrope stay lucid while in his monthly transformed state. The difficult brew prevents Lupin from becoming a danger to the castle's inhabitants during the full moon.

In 1994, the Hogwarts teachers have their hands full when the school hosts the Triwizard Tournament. It's safe to say Hagrid probably helps arrange for the dragons to be used during the first task, and Dumbledore is likely a vital part of the second task, since he can speak Mermish. For the third task, a gigantic hedge maze is erected on the Quidditch pitch, most likely with the help of Professor Sprout. The creatures inside the maze, including the Blast-Ended Skrewts, sphinx and Acromantula, are probably Hagrid's contribution, while the gold mist that leaves Harry hanging upside down is likely one of Flitwick's enchantments.

At the end of the 1997-1998 school year, the Hogwarts staff shows what they're made of during the Battle of Hogwarts, using their unique skills to protect the school and its inhabitants.

When Headmaster Snape flees as Voldemort approaches the school, Professor McGonagall takes charge of Hogwarts and defends it with the help of her colleagues. Flitwick helps put up protective barriers around the grounds to keep the Death Eaters out as long as they can. Meanwhile, Filch and Pomfrey evacuate the students who aren't taking part in the battle. Professor Sprout makes use of some dangerous plants to aid their defense, including mandrakes, Devil's Snare, Venomous Tentacula and Snargaluff pods. Professor Trelawney also does her part, dropping crystal balls on Death Eaters, taking out Fenrir Greyback in the process.

Meanwhile, Snape keeps close to the school so he can reveal to Harry that in order for Voldemort to be defeated, Harry must sacrifice himself. After Nagini fatally attacks Snape on Voldemort's orders, Snape manages to give Harry the final memories he needs to defeat Voldemort before succumbing to his injuries.

CHAPTER 2

COURSES AT HOGWARTS

Alchemy

Alchemy is an ancient branch of study, even older than Hogwarts School of Witchcraft and Wizardry. It has been practiced around the world, most notably in China, France and Egypt. This magical subject may have been offered at the school from its very beginnings given that it has been studied by prolific wizards such as Merlin and Albus Dumbledore. Despite its legendary practitioners, it is not widely studied by Hogwarts students in the 1990s, although other magical schools such as Uagadou in Africa are well-known for offering such coursework.

HISTORY OF ALCHEMY COURSE

Regarded by the Muggle community as an ancient branch of philosophy and science (bordering on pseudoscience), alchemy is viewed as a forerunner to modern chemistry. Although many of its figures contributed to the Muggle world's understanding of nature, these individuals have been relegated to the margins of history. For example, Muggle children are familiar with Sir Isaac Newton's first law of motion, though few learn that most of his academic pursuits centered on alchemy. Nicolas Flamel is a well-known figure among Muggles, who believe he failed to create a philosopher's stone and thus died within a normal lifetime.

In the magical community, alchemy is a very real branch of magic and science, and it is still studied and practiced by clever witches and wizards whose interests extend to the interaction between various elements. Alchemists often refer to ancient manuscripts as they seek explanations of mysterious phenomena and strive to produce magical substances, from moderate cures to the elusive Elixir of Life.

Alchemical processes appear in advanced practice within common disciplines such as potion-making and herbology. One can use knowledge of alchemy to investigate a blended poison and then produce an antidote (e.g., a bezoar, according to Snape). A less common practice is spagyric, developed by Paracelsus, in which wizards seek to manipulate plants rather than metals. Spagyric is mainly used for healing magical illnesses.

Students of alchemy are focused on three pursuits: finding or creating a Sorcerer's Stone, achieving eternal youth or life and transforming common metals into gold and silver. Of the three, alchemy is most widely associated with the philosopher's stone, since this substance alone can help an individual attain the other two goals. This field of magic also includes secondary pursuits, such as the search for a "panacea," a universal cure against all disease, and the practice of spagyric.

Though it's possible the four founders considered offering the subject as early as the first year, Alchemy is ultimately an advanced elective area of study offered only to sixth- and seventh-year (N.E.W.T.-level) Hogwarts students with a special interest in and aptitude for the subject. Lessons might only be offered if there is sufficient interest among students in this branch of magic for the given school year.

It is unclear whether students must achieve a certain O.W.L. grade in any related subjects before they may take up the specialized study of alchemy, but it can be speculated that only those students with Exceeds Expectations (if not Outstanding) marks in the following subjects would be admitted:

- **Ancient Runes**
- **Astronomy**
- **Herbology**
- **History of Magic**
- **Potions**
- **Transfiguration**

Outside of a specific Alchemy class, the topic appears in the curriculum of related subjects such as sixth-year Potions. The subject must be introduced somewhere between second and fifth year in order for it to spark the interest of students by the time they select their N.E.W.T. classes. Historical discoveries and figures in the field of alchemy are likely featured in History of Magic sometime after the first year, and it is possible the subject is also mentioned in Transfiguration, Astronomy and Herbology. Ancient Runes students might also be assigned to examine alchemical manuscripts.

NOTABLE ALCHEMY PROFESSORS AND STUDENTS

Although Harry Potter and his friends don't attend a lesson on alchemy before leaving Hogwarts to hunt Horcruxes in 1997, they encounter the topic during their first year when researching **Nicolas Flamel.** Despite the fact that **Hermione** clearly displays knowledge of and interest in the subject at the tender age of 12, she does not go on to seize the opportunity to study Alchemy at N.E.W.T. level. This could be because Hermione does not possess an ambition for achieving immortality or wealth, or it could be because she does not find the topic useful in the war against Voldemort.

It is unclear which Hogwarts professors teach N.E.W.T. students who wish to study alchemy, but there are some clues. In 1997, when **Horace Slughorn** is teaching his sixth-year Potions students about Golpalott's Third Law, he describes one particular assignment as a transformative process akin to alchemy. **Severus Snape**'s annotated copy of *Advanced Potion-Making* does not offer Harry clarification on Golpalott's Third Law; this suggests that, as a student, Snape understood these principles well enough without needing additional notes. Given these details, it's possible both Potions Masters have studied and might even teach the subject of Alchemy.

Other than Potions, another subject that has crossover with Alchemy is Transfiguration. Therefore, it is surmisable that Transfiguration professors **Albus Dumbledore** and **Minerva McGonagall** might offer such lessons. In fact, one of the feats Dumbledore is most famous for is his work on alchemy alongside his partner, Nicolas Flamel. Since Dumbledore, like Snape, has been known to give private lessons, it is reasonable that students of Alchemy might learn from him.

Given **Tom Riddle**'s extreme measures toward achieving immortality, including making early plans to create seven Horcruxes and succeeding in making two as a teenager, it is entirely possible he would've chosen to study

Alchemy at Hogwarts. He could then recall this knowledge while aspiring to steal Nicolas Flamel's Sorcerer's Stone and use it to regain his full strength during the 1991–1992 school year.

Another Hogwarts student who has an interest in alchemy is **Draco Malfoy**. As an adult, he possesses an interest in his collection of inherited alchemical manuscripts. Malfoy could have studied Alchemy as a N.E.W.T. student at Hogwarts, translating his studies into a hobby after school and the war.

REQUIRED ALCHEMY TEXTBOOKS BY YEAR

The textbooks required for sixth- and seventh-year students studying Alchemy are unknown, but the Hogwarts library contains several books on the subject. Many of these are presumably stored within the Restricted Section, where younger students would not be able to access them. This could be Dumbledore's doing, since by 1991 the headmaster and former alchemist had come to value the desire to protect the Stone over the use of it (and that being rich and immortal was not the noblest of pursuits). He likely would not approve of the broader school population having easy access to such learning material, especially after Tom Riddle's inquiries about Horcruxes at such a young age about 50 years prior.

Still, Hermione Granger manages to check out an enormous old book from the library that contains an excerpt concerning alchemy and Nicolas Flamel's success with creating the Sorcerer's Stone. This may have been *Alchemy, Ancient Art and Science* by Argo Pyrites, a book known to contain information on alchemy and the Stone.

Students of Alchemy might study copies of ancient manuscripts, while the originals might be lost, protected by historians, or else kept within ancient and powerful magical families like the Malfoys. One such manuscript could be the famous Ripley Scroll of the 15th century; it is 20 feet long and provides instructions for creating the philosopher's stone. The manuscript also contains numerous symbolic illustrations and poetry.

The principles of alchemy may be read about within assigned texts for other subjects, including *Advanced Potion-Making* by Libatius Borage, which is required reading for N.E.W.T.-level Potions. Borage discusses alchemy in the section on Golpalott's Third Law and preparing antidotes for blended poisons.

It can be assumed that Nicolas Flamel is not mentioned in *A History of Magic* by Bathilda Bagshot and other assigned textbooks for first-year students since Harry, Ron and Hermione have some difficulty combing through books for the name during the 1991–1992 academic year, but it's likely that higher-level reading for History of Magic would include alchemy and related figures.

DESCRIPTION OF ALCHEMY CLASSROOM

Unlike many subjects known to be taught at Hogwarts, it is unknown where students study alchemy. In 1995, a bust of famous alchemist Paracelsus can be found along a passage between the Gryffindor common room and the owlery. If the bust was near where theoretical and historical alchemy could be studied, then this would place an Alchemy classroom somewhere near the Fat Lady's portrait on the seventh floor of the castle. A chalkboard, professor's podium and rows of student desks for reading and writing would be necessary for lessons on theory and history. The height of this classroom would allow for ample light for perusing manuscripts and books.

Given the connection between the subject and Potions, it's possible practical lessons are given in the Potions classroom or nearby down in the dungeons of Hogwarts, with easy access to tools and materials needed for alchemical magic. Such tools might include desks, scales for measuring ingredients, cauldrons for brewing alchemical concoctions (such as the one in which Slughorn keeps Felix Felicis during Harry's sixth-year Potions class) and a chalkboard for displaying notes and instructions. Supplies such as base metals, liquids and plants could be locked in storage cabinets, and pure gold and silver might be made available so that students may study their properties in class. Aside from wands, students could use knives, a mortar and pestle, and other laboratory tools for manipulating material.

FAMOUS ALCHEMISTS THROUGHOUT WIZARDING AND MUGGLE HISTORY

Of the numerous famous alchemists throughout history, plenty of whom were indeed witches or wizards practicing magic to achieve alchemical feats, a number of Muggles have also contributed to the field.

Hermes Trismegistus (unknown), considered by most to be the father of alchemy, was said to be the combination of Thoth, the Egyptian god of wisdom, and Hermes, the Greek messenger god. The modern symbol for medicine, the caduceus, which features two snakes winding around a winged staff, is derived from Hermes Trismegistus. His writings are believed to be the basis for most alchemical knowledge as well as the principles for studying magic, astrology and philosophy (aka Hermeticism).

Dzou Yen, also known as Zou Yan (340–c. 260 B.C.E.), was a prolific spiritual alchemist in China in the fourth century B.C.E. His teachings on polarity through the cosmic principles of yin and yang also contributed to the alchemic standard of five elements, or phases: earth, fire, metal, water and wood. As the father of Chinese scientific thought, Dzou Yen greatly influenced the development and study of medicine, philosophy and alchemy in China.

Khalid ibn Yazid (c. 668–704) was an Umayyad prince who studied alchemy in Egypt. He translated texts on alchemy from the library of Alexandria and introduced them to the Islamic world. The term "alchemy," from the Arabic article for "the," "al-," and the Greek name for Egypt, "Khemia" (which referred to the valley around the Nile River, or "the land of black earth"), owes its origins to Khalid ibn Yazid.

George Ripley (c. 1415–1490), associated with the famous Ripley Scroll, was an English alchemist. Later alchemists would study his writings, such as *The Compound of Alchemy; or, the Twelve Gates leading to the Discovery of the Philosopher's Stone*. Though it is unclear whether Ripley himself created the famous scroll, its symbolic illustrations provide instruction for making the Stone.

Cornelius Agrippa (1486-1535), a German wizard and alchemist, wrote many books about magic in the 16th century. He was imprisoned by Muggles who feared his work was nefarious in nature. His most important writing was *Three Books on Occult Philosophy*, which discussed not only alchemy but also astrology and Kabbalah, a school of esoteric thought in Judaism. Agrippa is known in the Muggle world for having had a familiar in the form of a black dog. He now has his own Chocolate Frog card, which is rather rare and much sought after by collectors.

Paracelsus (1493-1541), also known as Theophrastus von Hohenheim, was a Swiss astrologist, physician and alchemist during the Renaissance. He is known as the father of pharmaceuticals, notably for his study of mineral effects on the body and his theory on chemical remedies for various illnesses. A bust of Paracelsus can be found at Hogwarts, and he can also be found on Chocolate Frog cards.

Hennig Brand (c. 1630-1710), a German chemist, studied bodily fluids in his search for the secret to making a philosopher's stone. Through his alchemical pursuits, he became the first person known to discover and name an element: phosphorus.

Sir Isaac Newton (1642-1727) was a polymath with whom many Muggles are familiar, though few know that more of his writings focus on alchemy than physics, mathematics or theology. Newton even wrote his own instructions for creating a philosopher's stone that could turn any base metal into gold and cure any illness.

NICOLAS FLAMEL AND THE SORCERER'S STONE

French alchemist **Nicolas Flamel** (1326–1992) is the most famous wizard who practiced alchemy. According to Muggle legend, upon finding a mysterious text called *The Book of Abraham the Jew*, which contained many strange symbols, Flamel dedicated his life's work to exploring the manuscript's mysteries. He deciphered instructions for creating the Sorcerer's Stone and became the only individual known to succeed in this endeavor. With his Sorcerer's Stone, Flamel was able to produce the Elixir of Life, which he then used to prolong his and his wife Perenelle's lives from the 14th to the 20th century. They lived in Paris, France, through 600 years of history, including the Dark wizard Gellert Grindelwald's rise and fall.

It isn't until the early 1990s, when Lord Voldemort seeks the Stone, that Flamel decides he has lived a long enough life and no longer desires to continue making and using the Elixir of Life. The Sorcerer's Stone is first held within a secure vault within Gringotts Bank in London, but before a rare, attempted break-in to steal the Stone, it is removed and placed under the protection of Flamel's old partner, Albus Dumbledore. Several members of the Hogwarts staff are tasked with creating obstacles designed to stop anyone who seeks to remove the Stone from the castle. Dumbledore's spell ensures that someone who wants only to find the Stone—but not use it to create gold or the Elixir of Life—will succeed in obtaining it. Only Quirinus Quirrell (possessed by Voldemort) and Harry Potter get through all of these obstacles to reach the final stage with the Mirror of Erised, but it's Harry who succeeds in acquiring the Stone.

After Harry defeats Quirrellmort, the artifact is destroyed. Without the Stone and its elixir to sustain them, the Flamels welcome death by succumbing to their incredibly advanced age. No other Sorcerer's Stone has been known to exist, and presumably the secret to creating one died with Flamel.

ARTIFACTS AND OBJECTS CREATED USING ALCHEMY

The **Sorcerer's Stone** is a magical object that was created by Nicolas Flamel in the 14th century. The Stone could turn any base metal into pure gold through a phenomenon called chrysopoeia and could be used to create the Elixir of Life. Originally kept at Flamel's home in Paris, the Stone is eventually transferred to a vault in Gringotts, from which it is removed in 1991 and placed in a chamber below Hogwarts where Harry thwarts Lord Voldemort's plans to steal it in 1992. The Stone is destroyed shortly after these events.

The **Elixir of Life** is a potion that, when imbibed, will give one eternal youth. It does not prevent the drinker's body from aging, only preserving their life force so they cannot die. The recipe for this potion calls for the rare Sorcerer's Stone; thus, only Nicolas Flamel and his wife, Perenelle, are known to have consumed it. The Elixir of Life must be continuously made and ingested over time or else the drinker will eventually die. If contaminated, the elixir will become poisonous. This potion might be the panacea that alchemists sought over the centuries, a cure for all disease. The Elixir of Life can also be used to restore a weakened, disembodied soul. This is the purpose behind Lord Voldemort's quest to find the Sorcerer's Stone at Hogwarts during the 1991–1992 school year. While he intends to use the potion's restorative properties, Voldemort does not intend on becoming dependent on drinking this potion to preserve his life, preferring the use of Horcruxes instead.

Various antidotes to blended poisons can be created with alchemical processes, as discussed in Harry's sixth-year Potions curriculum. If a potion-maker is seeking to discover which components can be used to change disparate elements within such poisons, then an antidote may be produced. This is considered advanced magic for students, only to be introduced at N.E.W.T.-level Potions.

Silver and gold, two valuable and highly sought-after substances through the ages, are central to alchemy. Much of the work of alchemists is devoted to transforming base metals into silver and gold through a process called chrysopoeia, thus bringing the alchemist great wealth. The

Sorcerer's Stone is said to have this ability, though Nicolas Flamel is not known for completing this process.

The Ripley Scroll is a famous alchemical manuscript named after the alchemist George Ripley (though it is disputed whether Ripley himself created the original scroll). There are many copies of this manuscript in existence, although they are rarely unfurled (which is difficult, since the scrolls are 20 feet long, or roughly the height of a giraffe). The Ripley Scroll's illustrations, along with text known as "Verses upon the Elixir," provide symbolic instructions for making a philosopher's stone.

ALCHEMY AND POTIONS: WHAT'S THE DIFFERENCE?

Many who dabble in alchemy are also adept potion-makers. The two fields of magical study are intertwined yet distinct. Alchemists use potions and related substances and tools in their work, and one of the primary goals of alchemy is to create perhaps the rarest and most valuable potion in history, the Elixir of Life. However, not all potion-makers or even Potions Masters practice alchemy, which is reserved only for those with the most advanced knowledge and selective interests. While Muggles may scoff at the history of alchemy while celebrating various alchemists for their contributions to modern science, the magical community holds respect and awe for accomplished alchemists like Nicolas Flamel.

Ancient Runes

Ancient Runes are a form of writing used by witches and wizards hundreds of years ago. Runic alphabets are known to have been in use well into the 17th century. Given that Hogwarts was founded in the 10th century, at that time, such runes may have been commonly used. By this logic, the course may have been added to the curriculum later on, once runes fell out of use and became obsolete.

HISTORY OF ANCIENT RUNES COURSE

Ancient Runes has presumably been a class at Hogwarts for quite some time, but the exact date the school began offering the course is not known. It is also unclear whether Ancient Runes was ever part of the core curriculum at Hogwarts. By the 1990s, it is offered as an elective to students in their third year and above. This indicates it is not considered an essential part of magical education but more of an area of specialty.

Ancient Runes is a theory-based subject, with likely no use for practical wandwork or incantations. Instead, its coursework focuses on reading and translating runic texts, or runology. Students likely learn multiple runic alphabets as well as a rune numbering system, which consists of drawn depictions of magical creatures to represent different values:

0 - The Demiguise's ability to become invisible symbolizes the value of zero.
1 - The unicorn's singular horn represents the number one.
2 - The Graphorn's two sharp horns stand for the number two.
3 - The Runespoor is a tri-headed creature representing the number three.
4 - The color varieties of the Fwooper stand for the number four.
5 - The five-legged Quintaped symbolizes the number five.
6 - The salamander represents the number six, the same number

of hours they can survive out of a fire.

7 - An unknown creature represents the number seven.

8 - The Acromantula's eight eyes symbolize the number eight.

9 - The hydra and its nine heads represent the number nine.

NOTABLE ANCIENT RUNES PROFESSORS AND STUDENTS

In the 1990s, **Professor Bathsheda Babbling** teaches Ancient Runes at Hogwarts. Little is known about her, but like her colleagues, it can be assumed that she is a master in her field, possessing an immense knowledge of various runes and ancient languages.

In 1993, **Hermione Granger** begins taking Ancient Runes as an elective in her third year at Hogwarts. She receives an "O" for "Outstanding" on the 1996 O.W.L. examination and proceeds to study the subject at N.E.W.T. level. Hermione later succeeds in translating *The Tales of Beedle the Bard* from the runic alphabet to modern English. Hermione's copy of the book was bequeathed to her in Albus Dumbledore's will. As the longtime owner of the book, it is reasonable to assume Dumbledore also studied runes or could at least read them.

Two Weasley brothers are known to have attended Ancient Runes class while at school: **Bill and Percy Weasley** each earned an O.W.L. in the subject. As a curse breaker for Gringotts Bank, Bill Weasley's knowledge of ancient magical languages likely comes in handy.

Barty Crouch, Jr., is also assumed to have studied Ancient Runes while at Hogwarts. According to his father, Crouch, Jr., earned 12 O.W.L. passing grades, which means he must have taken all the courses offered to students under their sixth year at Hogwarts, including Ancient Runes.

Xenophilius Lovegood may have also taken Ancient Runes while at school. The editor of *The Quibbler* publishes runic texts in an edition of his magazine. His daughter, Luna Lovegood, also may have an understanding of runes since she is seen reading this edition of *The Quibbler*.

REQUIRED ANCIENT RUNES TEXTBOOKS BY YEAR

Advanced Rune Translation (author unknown) is, as its title indicates, an advanced text for translating Ancient Runes. While it's not known if this book is included on reading lists for the class, Hermione purchases a copy in Diagon Alley prior to her sixth year at Hogwarts.

Ancient Runes Made Easy (author unknown) is a beginner's guide to runic alphabets. While it is not known if this is a required text for the course, if it is, it is likely recommended for third-year students first taking up the subject. Hermione Granger reads through this book in her second year at Hogwarts shortly after deciding to take Ancient Runes as an elective the following school year.

A rune dictionary (author unknown) is known to exist, but the official title is unknown. It could be that this dictionary is actually Spellman's Syllabary. Whether its own entity or just a reference to the Syllabary, the dictionary is used by Hermione in her third year onward. It's unknown if a dictionary was required or just recommended to complete Ancient Runes coursework. Though not an Ancient Runes student, Harry also finds a use for a rune dictionary in his fourth year while practicing the Summoning Charm ahead of the Triwizard Tournament. He succeeds in summoning the heavy book to him in the Gryffindor common room.

Magical Hieroglyphs and Logograms (author unknown) is a text used by Hermione in her fifth year at Hogwarts. She uses this book in combination with an assortment of other texts to work on her Ancient Runes homework. Like other Ancient Runes textbooks, it is unknown if this book is required reading for the class.

Spellman's Syllabary (author unknown) is used by fifth- and sixth-year students to translate Ancient Runes homework. Hermione uses it for homework and later to translate a copy of *The Tales of Beedle the Bard*.

DESCRIPTION OF ANCIENT RUNES CLASSROOM

It is unknown where inside Hogwarts the Ancient Runes classroom is located or what it might look like. However, speculation can help piece together a picture of the space.

Ancient Runes is, by nature, a theory-based subject. Students are studying a writing system from several hundred years ago; therefore, they need desks at which to read and write. Unlike a subject such as Defense Against the Dark Arts, however, space for the practical application of magic is not necessary. It is reasonable to assume that the room appears like any other traditional classroom, with rows of wooden desks facing a blackboard where examples of runes and their meanings could be displayed and closely examined.

When translating runes, students would need access to textbooks and reference guides. The walls might be lined with floor-to-ceiling bookshelves containing useful material for coursework.

A HISTORY OF RUNES IN EUROPE

In the Muggle world, runes were in use throughout Europe from around the third century into the 16th or 17th century to record data, mark personal belongings and communicate prior to the adoption of the Latin alphabet.

Developed by ancient Germanic-speaking peoples, runes were inscribed into wood, rock and metal and have been found across Northern Europe, Scandinavia, Britain and Iceland. Recognized by characteristically slanting lines, each symbol represents a sound in speech or, sometimes, a whole word. Runic sentences can be written from left to right or from right to left.

Various runic alphabets exist, with some evolving over time to account for changes in spoken languages. Elder Futhark is recognized as the oldest identified runic alphabet, thought to have been in use from the third to seventh centuries. Elder Futhark consists of 24 characters and is one of the alphabets studied by Hogwarts students.

After c. 700 CE, Elder Futhark was adapted into Younger Futhark, the alphabet used to write Old Norse during the Viking Age. The new iteration of runic text dropped eight of the original characters from the Elder Futhark alphabet. Younger Futhark consists of 16 characters, with each character standing for multiple speech sounds.

While the Scandinavian runic alphabet shrunk its character count, in Britain and Frisia (modern-day Netherlands), more symbols were added. The Anglo-Saxon Futhorc alphabet consists of 33 characters and was used to write Old English and Old Frisian. It is Anglo-Saxon Futhorc runes that appear etched around the basin of the Pensieve in Albus Dumbledore's office.

Runes were put to practical, everyday use for hundreds of years, but they also have a touch of mystique about them. Their origins are a bit of a mystery, and historians struggle to agree on when exactly runes began to turn up and from which prior alphabet they are derived. Legends and folklore explain their mysterious beginnings as divine intervention, not a mortal invention.

Nordic people believed that runes came directly from Odin, chief of the Norse gods. Legend has it that Odin speared himself to a tree as a self-sacrifice to gain knowledge of the occult. After nine days, he was given insight into runes, which he then passed on to his people. This belief that the runic alphabet is a divine gift from a god contributed to the idea that runes hold magical properties.

Ancient legends and poems from the Viking era mention various magical uses for runes such as spell-casting, protective charms and divination. Viking runemasters were said to have such thorough knowledge of the runic alphabet that they were able to employ it for magical purposes, writing inscriptions that could heal or protect. Examples include charms hung over beds to cure illness and drinking vessels inscribed to prevent the drinker from falling prey to poisoning. Viking warriors would often carry runic spells with them into battle. Shields would be inscribed with spells to protect their carriers, while swords would carry curses asking the gods to strike down their enemies. Similarly, medieval sagas report "victory runes" being engraved on the swords of soldiers heading into battle as well as runes being used to facilitate childbirth and to guide ships through a safe voyage.

There is also a long history of runes being used for divination purposes. In 98 CE, the Roman historian Tacitus wrote about how the Germanic people used runes as a means of seeing the future. According to Tacitus, runes would be written on pieces of wood and tossed onto a white cloth, and then three would be selected at random and their meanings interpreted. This process is called rune casting.

Modern practitioners use stones or ceramic tiles with symbols engraved or painted on them. Professor Trelawney attempts to demonstrate this method in the 1995–1996 school year.

RUNES FOUND AT HOGWARTS

Modified Saxon runes are present on the Pensieve in the headmaster's office when Harry visits it on several occasions. This artifact has been used by the many headmasters and headmistresses of Hogwarts. From the Anglo-Saxon alphabet, Saxon runes were used as an Old English writing system. The runes carved into the Pensive can provide information about when it was created.

The subject of Ancient Runes is mentioned in the copy of *The Quibbler* Luna Lovegood reads on the Hogwarts Express en route to Hogwarts in 1995. An article titled "Secrets of the Ancient Runes Revealed" is listed on the cover. It recommends turning the runes pictured in the article upside down to show a spell that would transform an enemy's ears into kumquats.

While being observed by Professor Umbridge during Harry's fifth year at the school, Professor Trelawney tries to demonstrate her skills in a variety of methods of divination, including the use of rune stones, to maintain her position as professor of Divination at Hogwarts. Unfortunately, her efforts do not persuade Umbridge, who attempts to remove her from the grounds.

When taking the O.W.L. exam for the subject in 1996, Hermione accidentally mixes up two runes in her translations: *eihwaz* and *ehwaz*. At Hogwarts, *eihwaz* means "defense" while *ehwaz* means "partnership." Both runes are derived from the Elder Futhark alphabet. In the alphabet, *ehwaz* means "horse" while *eihwaz* is derived from the Proto-Germanic word for "yew." It's likely the defense meaning came from the rune's use in divination or the connotation that yew wands complement protectors.

As noted, the copy of **The Tales of Beedle the Bard** Dumbledore leaves Hermione in his will is written in runes. While looking at the book with Hermione, Harry uses the term "rune" to refer to the Deathly Hallows symbol before the trio knows what it is. Hermione, however, states it is not a rune and does not appear in her copy of **Spellman's Syllabary.**

PRACTICAL AND EVERYDAY RUNES VS. ANCIENT RUNES

Ancient Runes covers old written languages, so it's likely that runes used today could look very different from those developed thousands of years ago. Even those mentioned during Harry's time at Hogwarts, like *eihwaz* and *ehwaz*, have been adapted from their original forms. That doesn't necessarily mean everyday and practical runes are unrecognizable from their ancient counterparts, but there could be variations in the runes taught in the course and practical ones used today.

Students taking Ancient Runes learn how to translate and read texts based on rune-based languages that are not actively used today. If these practical and everyday runes are taught at Hogwarts, it would likely be in the form of how they're used, both on their own and in conjunction with other forms of magic.

Practical rune use may involve using modern runes to perform magic or divination. The runes used by Professor Trelawney in a Divination lesson during the 1995–1996 school year are on stones, which may be how ancient runes were once used as well. Rather than using runes as a written language for communication, such practical runes could be used to defog the future or in other areas of prophesying. It's also possible practical runes are used to amplify the power or effectiveness of spells once cast.

If these types of runes are used to complete everyday tasks or in conjunction with spell-casting, this may only be a practice in certain wizarding cultures or settlements. This may explain why they aren't taught at Hogwarts, since the populations that the school's students come from may not be a part of the wizarding societies that use them. If practical and everyday runes are taught at Hogwarts, they would likely be studied in their own course. Depending on course enrollment numbers, however, it might not be considered reasonable or feasible to have two separate elective courses on similar subjects, and it could also be argued practical rune use is covered in Divination, not warranting a separate course on the topic. That isn't to say their use isn't potentially included in the curriculums of other wizarding schools.

Another explanation for why practical and everyday runes aren't included in the Hogwarts curriculum as a subject may be how they're interpreted in society. Everyday runes may be seen in a negative light, only being used by people who are "different." Hermione called Divination a "woolly" subject, and the same may be thought of those who use modern runes. If relying on everyday and practical runes in wizarding society is looked down on, it may explain why the subject isn't taught at Hogwarts, or why more isn't known on the subject in the modern magical community.

Arithmancy

The word "arithmancy," a magical subject first studied by the Greeks, derives from the Ancient Greek *arithmos*, meaning "number," and *manteia*, meaning "divination." Arithmancy is often described as an ancient form of divination, but unlike the subject of Divination (see pg. 107), which entails analyzing dreams and visions, Arithmancy relies on numbers to make predictions (which is why some consider it more reliable). Arithmancers allocate numbers to each letter of the alphabet to discover people's destiny numbers and use basic mathematical methods to determine an individual's life and birth paths.

HISTORY OF ARITHMANCY COURSE

Arithmancy has likely been a part of the curriculum at Hogwarts for many years. It is unknown whether or not Arithmancy was one of the required core courses for students at any point in the school's history, but it is unlikely since Arithmancy is a pretty advanced subject. In the 1990s, it is one of the elective courses made available to third-year students.

Arithmancy uses numbers to predict the future and contains elements of numerology. Numerology is the art of assigning a numerical value to letters or words, with the intention of using those numbers to understand life or world events. There are several different types of numbers that can be calculated, such as a life path number or a destiny number.

Based on descriptions of the course, students taking Arithmancy are expected to understand different numerical charts and calculations. These charts may show how numerology is used in different modern and dead languages, with numerical values assigned to the characters in each alphabet. Other languages that may be used include Latin, different forms of Old English, and modern languages. In addition to learning about how numerology is used in other languages, there are several different types of numerology that students may learn about. There are four main methods used in numerological calculations: Chaldean, Kabbalah, Tamil and Western. It's unknown which of these Hogwarts students learn about, if any, but they likely learn about at least one of them.

Arithmancy is required for those interested in pursuing a career in curse breaking, meaning such students must achieve passing O.W.L. and N.E.W.T. scores. Based on the number of students pursuing the career, it's probably not the most popular elective course to take but nonetheless retains the number of students necessary to justify teaching the subject each year.

How Arithmancy Is Used Today

Now commonly referred to as numerology, arithmancy still has its place in the modern world. People use numerology to learn more about their own personality traits, relationships with others, and the people around them. Mostly, they engage in it just for fun. It is no longer a subject that is seriously studied by many.

In Arithmancy, every number has a special meaning

0 - comprehensiveness and openness
1 - creation and leadership
2 - the peacemaker
3 - creativity
4 - strength and stability
5 - daring and independent
6 - loving and caring
7 - intellectual explorer
8 - power and balance
9 - loving and empathetic

BASIC FORMULAS
THE PYTHAGOREAN METHOD

This is the most popular method used in arithmancy to determine destiny numbers. It makes use of the modern Latin alphabet and assigns the numbers one to nine to each letter, starting at one again after nine. A destiny number is then calculated by adding up the numbers of a person's full name and then reducing it to a single digit.

1	2	3	4	5	6	7	8	9
A	B	C	D	E	F	G	H	I
J	K	L	M	N	O	P	Q	R
S	T	U	V	W	X	Y	Z	

REDUCING NUMBERS TO A SINGLE DIGIT

This is the most basic and widely used formula in arithmancy to calculate life and birth paths, among other details. The method is straightforward: Always reduce numbers to a single digit, except if that number is a master number, of which there are three: 11, 22, and 33.

For example, to reduce the number 237:
- **Treat each numeral as a single digit, then add up the numbers:** 2 + 3 + 7 = 12
- **12 is still a double digit, and it's not a master number, so we would reduce it further:** 1 + 2 = 3

In this example, **three** is the final number of the calculation, and as mentioned on the previous page, it represents creativity.

NOTABLE ARITHMANCY PROFESSORS AND STUDENTS

Professor Septima Vector is a witch who teaches Arithmancy at Hogwarts from at least 1993 through 1997. It is likely she is an accomplished arithmancer given her position as a professor. Due to her choice of profession, it is almost guaranteed she took Arithmancy at an advanced level as part of her education.

Hermione begins taking Arithmancy during the 1993–1994 school year, using a Time-Turner to attend the course because it sometimes conflicts with Care of Magical Creatures or Divination. Hermione is well accomplished in the subject, earning an Outstanding on the O.W.L. exam, and lists it as one of her favorite classes.

Bill Weasley, the eldest Weasley child, excelled in Arithmancy. The subject is a required course for curse breakers, and this academic success helped pave the way for his career at Gringotts. His younger brother Percy also achieves an O.W.L. in the subject.

REQUIRED ARITHMANCY TEXTBOOKS BY YEAR

New Theory of Numerology (author unknown) is a book Harry gifts to Hermione for Christmas in 1995. Because it's a gift and not purchased for school, it is likely a recommended textbook or leisurely reading material. It may contain information considered too advanced for the Hogwarts curriculum or expand on topics discussed in the course.

Numerology and Gramatica (author unknown) is a textbook Hermione uses while taking Arithmancy in her third year. While it is unclear whether or not this is a required textbook, it's likely to be at the very least recommended reading for the course. The text probably contains information on the different types of numbers used in the subject and the different types of methods that could be used to calculate them. In 1997, Hermione considers taking this text on the trio's hunt for Horcruxes.

DESCRIPTION OF ARITHMANCY CLASSROOM

It is not known where the Arithmancy classroom is or what it looks like. Based on what is known about the subject, however, necessary materials and a basic layout can be speculated. Like other classrooms, it's probable there are rows of wooden desks. Perhaps there are larger tables to encourage collaboration.

Based on the subject material, it is likely the classroom contains at least one chalkboard that can be used to write out numerical equations and sequences. There may also be other boards or large pieces of parchment lining the walls displaying numerical charts on them for easy reference.

Other reference materials like books and charts may be available for use in the classroom. These materials may be divided by language or method for accessibility. Perhaps calculating tools, such as an abacus, are available.

LIFE PATHS AND BIRTH PATHS, EXPLAINED

In arithmancy, a life path number is calculated by adding up the numbers of a birth date and then reducing it to a single digit or master number. A birth path simply refers to the day someone was born and usually indicates the talents a person possesses.

HARRY POTTER
Birthday 7/31/1980
Life Path Number 11
Birth Path Number 31

Eleven is a master number. Master numbers are associated with struggle and great achievements. In general, they tend to harbor heavy energy, which means people with this life path number will learn hard lessons that will reveal their potential. Eleven is seen as one of the most intuitive numbers in arithmancy and typically suggests that a person is very sensitive, almost to the point where they display psychic abilities. This pretty much describes Harry's life path to a T. Growing up without parents and living with the Dursleys proves challenging, but in the end, he manages to defeat Lord Voldemort. It can also be argued that his scar, which provides him with glimpses into Voldemort's mind, functions in a psychic capacity.

Harry's birth path number is 31, which represents creativity and determination but also stubbornness when it comes to stepping out of one's comfort zone. Though he leads students in Dumbledore's Army in defensive spellwork lessons, when confronting attackers, he prefers using the Disarming Charm above all other spells because he's most comfortable with it. He tends to use his creativity most when it comes to getting himself and his friends out of sticky situations.

RON WEASLEY
Birthday 3/1/1980
Life Path Number 22
Birth Path Number 1

Ron also has a master number life path: 22, meaning he faces struggles and learns hard lessons while growing up. This is considered the most powerful number in arithmancy and indicates the person in question is set to do great things during their lifetime. Ron also faces his share of teenage tribulations: He is teased about receiving his

siblings' hand-me-downs and feels he has to live up to his older brothers' achievements while often living in Harry's shadow. Ron learns important lessons during his time at Hogwarts, especially during the trio's hunt for Horcruxes, and in the end, he plays a vital role in defeating Voldemort.

Ron's birth path number signifies leadership qualities and a hunger for success. Ron shows signs of both: When he looks into the Mirror of Erised in 1991, he sees himself as head boy and holding the Quidditch Cup. Years later, he is made a prefect, like his brothers before him.

HERMIONE GRANGER
Birthday 9/19/1979
Life Path Number 9
Birth Path Number 19

Hermione's life path number is nine, which means she cares a lot about the world and the people around her, especially those who cannot stand up for themselves. Nines are also incredibly compassionate and idealistic. While they can be pretty hard on themselves and severely disappointed by the realities of life, nines are also very creative and use this skill to try to make the world a better place. Hermione cares deeply about the injustices of the magical community and founds S.P.E.W. (the Society for the Promotion of Elfish Welfare) to create awareness of the limited rights of house-elves. She is also incredibly hard on herself, occasionally fretting over small things like getting a question wrong on a test or worrying she hasn't studied enough.

Hermione's birth path number indicates unmatched determination and a desire for independence. She goes the extra mile, using a Time-Turner to take all her subjects during the 1993–1994 school year, and always takes the initiative to achieve her goals.

DRACO MALFOY
Birthday 6/5/1980
Life Path Number 11
Birth Path Number 5

With a master life path number of 11, Draco endures various adversities throughout his life but is also set to achieve great things. Growing up as the only child of Lord Voldemort devotees could not have been easy for Draco, especially given his particularly cold father. He has the capacity to achieve great things—which he does by sneaking Death Eaters into the school right under Dumbledore's nose. While that is most certainly not an achievement that's worth praising, it indicates Draco has the potential to achieve near-impossible feats.

Draco's birth path number suggests he is an adventurer with a deep-seated desire to be free. Fives can be very persuasive but also stubborn and overly confident. Draco displays some of these traits: Growing up with Lucius must have made him want to escape a fate tied to Voldemort, and he is skilled at convincing people (like Crabbe and Goyle) to stick by his side and do his bidding.

TOM RIDDLE
Birthday 12/31/1926
Life Path Number 7
Birth Path Number 31

Sevens are philosophers and seekers of truth. They usually stand out among their peers and tend to be misunderstood. They're typically not cheerful and often battle with existential questions. As a young adult, Tom Riddle most certainly experienced some sort of existential crisis—after all, no one creates seven Horcruxes to escape mortality on a whim. He was very much a loner most of his life and was curious about rare, dark branches of magic.

Like Harry, Riddle's birth path number is 31. This number indicates that a person is creative and disciplined and always tries to make the most of what they have at their disposal. They are stubborn, determined, and tenacious. Riddle displays these characteristics in his search for and creation of Horcruxes as well as his constant hunt for the Boy Who Lived after coming into his own as Lord Voldemort.

SEVERUS SNAPE
Birthday 1/9/1960
Life Path Number 8
Birth Path Number 9

Often referred to as "the great Karmic equalizer," those whose life path is an eight have the power to destroy and create in equal measure. Positive traits include being loving and having strong leadership qualities. Eights, however, also tend to become easily angered and frustrated and can harbor hate toward those who did them wrong, qualities that Severus Snape has in great supply. While he displays a great capacity for love and strong leadership qualities (both Voldemort and Albus Dumbledore trust him with their lives), he also permits what happened in his past to cloud his logic and make him bitter.

Snape's birth path number, nine, is associated with creativity. Nines tend to pursue a higher purpose and have great gut instincts they use to guide themselves throughout life. On the downside, they can hold grudges, especially when they feel justice hasn't been served. Snape displays plenty of these characteristics: He holds a lifelong grudge against James Potter and his friends, often taking out his anger on James's son, Harry. But Snape also possesses a keen intuition, which leads him to join Dumbledore after fleeing Voldemort's ranks. This also serves him well when working as a double agent to bring Voldemort and his followers down.

Astronomy

Humans have been fascinated with mapping and understanding celestial objects for thousands of years. Documented efforts to practice astronomy date back to 1,000 B.C.E. by the Assyro-Babylonians. In the magical community, centaurs also take a keen interest in plotting the movements of stars, planets and other astronomical objects, from which they draw insights about the world.

HISTORY OF ASTRONOMY COURSE

Since it's an ancient field of study, it's safe to say astronomy has been taught at Hogwarts since the school's inception. As one of the few subjects at Hogwarts that coincide with what is taught in the Muggle world, it might also be possible for wizards to keep tabs on discoveries made by NASA and other space administrations. Astronomy at Hogwarts familiarizes students with the planets and their moons, as well as stars and constellations.

During Harry's time at Hogwarts, students even learn detailed information about Jupiter and its moons that were discovered by Muggle spacecrafts, studying the various moons' surfaces and sizes. Ron also draws Io, a volcanic moon that orbits Jupiter, relying on visual data that Muggles obtained via space exploration. Io is notably not visible in detail when using Earth-bound telescopes. Unless the telescopes wizards use are magically enhanced to observe the same things in space that spacecrafts do, Hogwarts's Astronomy class has borrowed its information and teachings from the Muggle world in the past and likely continues to do so to this day.

NOTABLE ASTRONOMY PROFESSORS AND STUDENTS

Astronomy is a compulsory subject at Hogwarts for the first five years. It is taught by **Professor Aurora Sinistra**, about whom little is known. She appears to be a rather serious witch. Outside the classroom, she is known to engage in school activities, such as attending meals, feasts and the Yule Ball, where she is seen dancing with Professor Alastor Moody.

To teach this subject at Hogwarts, it can be assumed Professor Sinistra must possess a vast knowledge of outer space and our solar system. Her classroom is located at the top of the Astronomy Tower, making it easy for students to explore the night skies with their telescopes. Professor Sinistra is most likely a night owl, given she teaches most of her classes at midnight when the stars and planets are at their most visible via telescope. She educates students on the mysteries of outer space, showing them the different constellations and stars, planets and moons.

During their first five years at the school, **Harry**, **Ron** and **Hermione** all take Astronomy. Harry and Ron are not as enthusiastic about the subject as Hermione. While they spend plenty of time studying the night skies, their homework requires them to draw star charts and write essays about planets and their moons, most notably Jupiter.

In his fifth year, Harry makes a blunder in his Astronomy essay when he writes that Europa is covered in mice rather than ice. Hermione catches the error as she looks over Harry's and Ron's homework. She also provides Ron with corrections for his essay and even writes a conclusion she has him copy out, indicating her proficiency in the subject.

Harry achieves an A (Acceptable) O.W.L. for the subject. Ron also achieves an O.W.L., but Hermione, of course, surpasses them both by receiving an O (Outstanding) O.W.L. **Percy**, who obtained 12 O.W.L.s, certainly fared well in Astronomy, as did his older brother **Bill**, who also obtained 12 O.W.L.s in his fifth year.

REQUIRED ASTRONOMY MATERIALS

Blank Star Charts Students use star charts in practical classes and examinations to make precise drawings of the celestial bodies they observe through their telescopes.

Parchment and Quills Astronomy requires students to study plenty of theory. Students apply this knowledge by writing lengthy essays, especially during their fifth year.

Reference Books No specific textbooks for Astronomy appear on students' school supplies list, but they do make use of reference books, as Hermione does during the 1995–1996 school year when she fact-checks Harry's and Ron's essays on Jupiter. These reference books likely include imagery of galaxies, nebulae and other astronomical objects.

Telescopes Each student must use a telescope to study the night sky during practical classes and examinations. Students can purchase telescopes in Diagon Alley or if necessary, borrow from the school's inventory as a backup. In 1991, for Harry's first year, he buys a collapsible brass telescope.

An orrery, a model of the solar system with movable parts that show the planets and their moons in orbit, isn't a required item but could be very useful. As a third-year student, Harry is tempted to buy one, since he's certain owning an orrery (and thereby consulting it whenever needed) means he'd never have to take an Astronomy class again.

DESCRIPTION OF ASTRONOMY CLASSROOM

Astronomy is taught in the tallest tower of Hogwarts, which is situated almost directly above the castle's front doors and is surrounded by a parapet. A steep spiral staircase leads to an iron-handled door, through which the top of the tower can be accessed. From there, a perfect view of the Hogwarts grounds and the sky above is available.

Although little is known about the exact layout of the tower, there is at least enough space for several students to set up their telescopes and spread out their star charts. It is likely that the space is not fully enclosed, a fact evidenced by a few different instances experienced by Harry.

During the 1991-1992 academic year, Charlie Weasley's friends are easily able to land at the tower and retrieve Hagrid's baby dragon from Harry. Since they're able to land their brooms, retrieve the baby dragon and take off again in a short amount of time, it's likely they're not restricted by doors or windows when accessing the tower.

In 1996, Harry describes the space as having "a slight chill in the air" as he and his classmates begin the practical portion of their O.W.L.s, which implies the space is open to the elements.

During the 1996-1997 school year, Harry and Dumbledore fly on broomsticks to the Astronomy Tower after noticing the Dark Mark above it. When they land, the space is described as deserted "crenelated ramparts" and there is a seemingly unobstructed view of the closed door that leads into the castle. Not long after they land, Harry watches in horror as Dumbledore is sent flying over the "battlements" after he is hit by the Killing Curse. Crenelated ramparts—also known as battlements—are walls with gaps at regular intervals surrounding the top of a castle or fortress. These gaps were traditionally used for firing weaponry to defend the structure during attacks. This confirms that the tower is not fully enclosed by walls, doors or windows, since nothing prevents Dumbledore from plummeting to the ground below.

THE INTERDISCIPLINARY IMPACT OF ASTRONOMICAL STUDIES

All students at Hogwarts are required to take Astronomy during their first year. Students ascend the steps of the Astronomy Tower and spend the night studying the names and movements of different stars and planets. While all mandatory subjects at Hogwarts serve a purpose, Astronomy is crucial for first years because so many of their other courses will require a foundational knowledge of the infinite, mysterious sky.

CARE OF MAGICAL CREATURES

The lunar cycle affects the mooncalf, a magical beast that only leaves its burrow during a full moon. During this time, the mooncalf performs complicated dance moves believed to be part of a mating ritual.

CELESTIAL OBJECTS & HEALING

Medieval Healing seems to have been influenced by the lunar cycle. In Harry's fifth year, the portrait of a medieval Healer at St. Mungo's Hospital for Magical Maladies and Injuries begins to explain that to cure the contagious disease known as Spattergroit, one can "take the liver of a toad, bind it tight about your throat, stand naked by the full moon in a barrel of eels' eyes —"

DIVINATION

When studying Divination, students are responsible for learning about astrology, which relies upon astronomical objects as a way to interpret and understand earthly happenings. According to Professor Trelawney, Mars causes accidents and burns, so when it makes an angle to Saturn, one must be careful when handling hot things. On its own, Saturn has a negative or threatening influence on a person if the planet is in a prominent position at the time of their birth. Some of these influences, according to Trelawney, might include dark hair, short height and tragic losses early in life. Trelawney also teaches that Pluto can disrupt everyday life. Throughout their divination studies, students are asked to make predictions based on this planetary information.

POTIONS

Knowledge of the lunar cycle is vital to brewing certain potions. For example, fluxweed must be picked during a full moon in order to brew a successful Polyjuice Potion. Similarly, Veritaserum requires one full moon cycle to mature into a finished potion. Wolfsbane Potion is brewed to be taken during the full moon (see Astronomy and Transformations on pg. 71).

HARRY POTTER

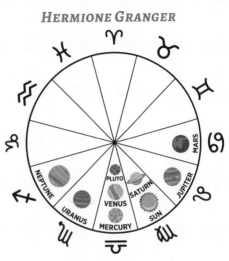

HERMIONE GRANGER

RON WEASLEY

STAR CHARTS

These maps of the night sky include the exact positions of stars, planets, constellations and galaxies at one point in time. Astrologers and astrology enthusiasts use a star chart from the exact moment of an individual's birth to analyze and interpret aspects of their life.

Because Pluto takes so long to orbit the sun, it spends 12 to 23 years in each zodiac sign. When Harry, Ron, and Hermione were born, Pluto was in Libra. According to astrologers, Libra rules balance and peace. Those with Pluto in Libra are thought to value love, justice and collective change.

ASTRONOMY AS IT RELATES TO WIZARD NAMES

There is no shortage of meaningful, interesting symbolism to be found within the names of characters within the magical world. Because of this, it isn't unusual to find names with etymological roots in astronomy or astrology.

THE BLACK FAMILY TRADITION

Many members of the Black family are named after stars, constellations, and moons. There are also several interesting relationships between various members of the family that correlate with their respective name origins.

Alphard Black Alphard is the brightest star in the constellation Hydra, which is often depicted as a water snake. Just northeast of Alphard is the brighter star, Regulus.

Andromeda Tonks (née Black) Andromeda is a constellation in the Northern Hemisphere referred to as "the Chained Maiden." This constellation also contains the Andromeda galaxy.

Arcturus Black I, II Arcturus is the brightest star in the constellation Boötes the Herdsman and the fourth-brightest star in the sky. Arcturus is derived from Ancient Greek Arktourus, meaning "bear guard." Greek mythology states that Zeus placed Arcturus in the sky to watch over Callisto and Arcas, who were turned into bears

DID YOU KNOW?

Astronomical or astrological influence can even be found in the names of animals, like the Abraxans that pull Beauxbatons's carriage, or certain job titles, such as Aurors for the Ministry of Magic. In Greco-Roman mythology, Abraxas is the name of a flying horse that pulls the sun god Helios's chariot through the sky. Similarly, the Abraxans that pull Beauxbatons's carriage are a breed of winged horses. The title of Auror may have been influenced by the natural light display seen in the sky on Earth or refer to the Roman goddess of the dawn.

and then placed into the constellations Ursa Major and Ursa Minor.

Bellatrix Lestrange (née Black) Bellatrix is the third-brightest star in the constellation Orion and the 25th-brightest star in the sky. It is one of the four "navigational stars" in Orion.

Cassiopeia Black Cassiopeia is a constellation in the Northern Hemisphere.

Cygnus Black I, II Cygnus is a constellation in the Northern Hemisphere; it is also known as the Northern Cross.

Delphini (daughter of Bellatrix Lestrange) Delphinus is a constellation in the northern sky, close to the celestial equator. Alpha Delphini is a main sequence star in the constellation.

Draco Malfoy (son of Narcissa Malfoy née Black) Draco is a constellation in the Northern Hemisphere.

Orion Black Orion is a constellation in the Northern Hemisphere known as Orion the Hunter.

Pollux Black Pollux is a star in the constellation Gemini.

Regulus Black I, II Regulus is the brightest star in the constellation Leo, and it is located at the heart of the lion depicted by those stars.

Scorpius Malfoy (grandson of Narcissa Malfoy née Black) Scorpius is a constellation in the Southern Hemisphere.

Sirius Black I, II, III Sirius is the brightest star in the constellation Canis Major (the Dog). Interestingly, Sirius's Animagus form is a large black dog.

Not all members of the Black family follow this astronomical tradition: Unlike her two sisters, Narcissa Malfoy (née Black) is named after a flower (or, arguably, a Greek god).

OTHER ASTRONOMICAL/ASTROLOGICAL ETYMOLOGY

There are few references to astronomy or astrology in the names of other known witches and wizards outside of the Black family.

Aurora Sinistra Aurora may refer to the well-known natural light display seen in the sky on Earth. It may also refer to the Roman goddess of the dawn. Sinistra is a star in the constellation Ophiuchus.

Cassandra Trelawney In Greek mythology, Cassandra was a prophetess who was gifted her ability by the sun god Apollo.

Firenze Firenze is the Italian name for the city of Florence, home to famous astronomer Galileo.

Luna Lovegood Luna, which means "moon" in Italian, Latin, Romanian, and Spanish, is also the name of the goddess of the moon in Roman mythology. The word "lunatic" is derived from "luna," because it was once believed that strange behavior correlated with moon cycles.

Remus Lupin "Lupin" is derivative of *lupus*, meaning "wolf" in Latin. Lupus is a constellation in the Southern Hemisphere.

Merope Gaunt Merope is a star in the Taurus constellation and a member of the Pleiades star cluster. According to Greek mythology, Merope was a nymph who was shamed for marrying a mortal man, causing her star to be the weakest in the Pleiades cluster.

> ### DID YOU KNOW?
> Claudius Ptolemy was an ancient astronomer who discovered the constellation Lupus and believed Earth to be the center of the universe. He was also a wizard and is now featured on collectible Chocolate Frog cards.

Rabastan Lestrange Rabastan is a star in the constellation Beta Draconis.

CENTAUR, MUGGLE AND WIZARD ASTRONOMY

There appears to be little difference between wizard and Muggle astronomy. Both versions of the discipline involve the study of the names, locations, and movements of stars, constellations, and planets.

While the centaur study of astronomical affairs also involves these basic tenets, centaurs view the idea of "reading the stars" as more than a hobby or a scientific pursuit, even using astronomy to predict the future (a practice known as astrology). For example, during the 1995–1996 school year, Divination professor and centaur Firenze admonishes Parvati Patil for believing Professor Trelawney's teachings that the position of planets affects trivial human behavior. He rejects this line of thinking, saying, "That is human nonsense. Trivial hurts, tiny human accidents. These are of no more significance than the scurrying of ants to the wide universe, and are unaffected by planetary movements." According to Firenze, centaurs have "unraveled the mysteries" of the planetary movements over centuries and have learned to interpret these movements in a way that can predict aspects of the future. Centaurs also claim that only their kind possesses this ability, believing that humans (wizard and Muggle alike) are limited by their very nature.

It would seem that astronomy and astrology are much more closely tied for centaurs than for wizards or Muggles. If Firenze's beliefs are in line with those of centaur culture at large, it could be argued centaurs only see astronomy as a means to an end, that end being prediction of the future.

ASTRONOMY AND TRANSFORMATIONS

Astronomy—specifically the lunar cycle—plays a large role in various forms of transformations within the magical community.

ANIMAGI

An Animagus is a wizard who can take the form of an animal. This extraordinarily rare ability cannot be achieved without first brewing an intricate potion with ties to the lunar cycle. The wizard must first place a single mandrake leaf in their mouth during the full moon and keep it there for one month. Once the second full moon arrives, the leaf must be placed in a crystal vial to receive "pure" moon rays until the remaining portions of the spell are complete.

WEREWOLVES

Like the werewolves of Muggle fiction, those afflicted with lycanthropy in the magical community are heavily influenced by the lunar cycle. Each month, on the full moon, they become ill and transform into their werewolf form. There is no cure for their ailment, but the Wolfsbane Potion, if taken in the week leading up to the full moon, allows a werewolf to retain their human mind when transformed.

Care of Magical Creatures

Unbeknownst to Muggles, the world is filled with magical creatures. Care of Magical Creatures seeks to familiarize students with the habits, habitats and life cycles of various animals and how to look after them or, at worst, avoid them. Students discover what these creatures eat, the habitats in which they can be found, the magical abilities or properties they may possess, and the diseases and illnesses that can affect them.

HISTORY OF CARE OF MAGICAL CREATURES COURSE

It is unknown when the subject of Care of Magical Creatures was first taught at Hogwarts. By the 1980s, the course is offered as an elective to students in their third year.

Students who pass the O.W.L. examination can choose to continue with the subject to the N.E.W.T. level or drop the class. During the 1995-1996 school year, the practical portion of the O.W.L. examination takes place on the castle lawn. Students are asked to identify a Knarl hidden among a bunch of ordinary hedgehogs. (Clever students know the trick is to offer each creature a drink of milk since only the Knarls take offense at the gesture.) The O.W.L. also requires students to demonstrate the proper handling of a Bowtruckle, feed and clean a Fire Crab without injury and identify the correct diet to feed a sick unicorn.

According to Dumbledore, Hogwarts students perform consistently well on Care of Magical Creatures examinations. He credits this to the thoroughness of Newt Scamander's work, *Fantastic Beasts and Where to Find Them*, which is required reading for the course.

Students who demonstrate an affinity for Care of Magical Creatures may pursue several different career paths, such as becoming a Magizoologist or working at the Ministry of Magic in offices related to magical creatures.

NOTABLE PROFESSORS AND STUDENTS

The Care of Magical Creatures course at Hogwarts was taught for a good many years by **Silvanus Kettleburn**. In 1993, Professor Kettleburn retires to "enjoy more time with his remaining limbs," as Dumbledore puts it.

His successor, **Rubeus Hagrid**, teaches the subject while simultaneously carrying out his duties as gamekeeper. Although he lacks a complete seven-year Hogwarts education (due to having been expelled decades prior), Hagrid's practical knowledge of magical creatures is likely what leads Dumbledore to offer him the job.

During the 1990s, **Wilhelmina Grubbly-Plank** stands in as a substitute teacher whenever Hagrid is away from his post. Professor Grubbly-Plank wins over students with her lessons on Bowtruckles and unicorns, with **Parvati Patil** even wishing she would stay on as the permanent instructor.

Harry, **Hermione** and **Ron** all take Care of Magical Creatures classes and pass the O.W.L. examination. The three later drop the subject following the conclusion of their fifth year. In fact, Harry and Hermione believe no one in their year decided to continue with the subject. This is likely due to Hagrid's reputation for bringing dangerous creatures to class for students to interact with.

Fred, **George**, **Percy**, **Bill** and **Charlie Weasley** all took Care of Magical Creatures while at Hogwarts. Both Percy and Bill passed the O.W.L. examination. **Angelina Johnson** also earns an O.W.L. in the subject.

While it remains unconfirmed, it can be assumed **Newt Scamander** took Care of Magical Creatures while at Hogwarts as his reputation as a famed Magizoologist suggests some prior training in the subject. Influenced by his mother's breeding of hippogriffs, Newt demonstrated a love for magical creatures from an early age. He went on to work at the Ministry of Magic, first in the Office for House-Elf Relocation and then in the Beast Division.

REQUIRED CARE OF MAGICAL CREATURES TEXTBOOKS BY YEAR

Fantastic Beasts and Where to Find Them by Newt Scamander has been a standard textbook required at Hogwarts since it was first published in 1927. By the 1930s, the book was also required reading for fifth-year students at Ilvermorny School in the United States. *Fantastic Beasts* provides detailed descriptions of magical creatures from around the world. Covering everything from Acromantulas to yetis, the book also notes the Ministry of Magic's classification (read: danger rating) for each creature. The rating is on a scale from one to five X's, with five being the most dangerous.

A former Hogwarts student himself, Newt Scamander was commissioned to write the book in 1918 for publisher Obscurus Books while working as an employee of the Ministry of Magic. After several years of field research, he collated his findings into what would eventually become an international best seller.

Although Harry, like any Hogwarts student, isn't permitted to sign up for Care of Magical Creatures until his third year, *Fantastic Beasts* is still listed as required reading for his first year and he purchases a copy in 1991. It can be assumed the book must have been required for more than one class at Hogwarts.

The Monster Book of Monsters (author unknown) is required reading in the 1993–1994 school year, assigned by Hagrid, who finds it amusing that the book attacks anyone who tries to read it. The cover is made from green leather, with the title emblazoned in gold. To open it without injury, readers must stroke the spine. When Hagrid sends Harry a copy for his 13th birthday, Harry fastens a belt around it to keep it from biting him.

Flourish and Blotts keeps its copies of the book in an iron cage. While this protects potential buyers from injury, it doesn't prevent the books from engaging in wrestling matches and ripping out each other's pages. When Harry visits the store prior to his third year, a store manager has to don protective gloves and wield a stick in order to retrieve copies for Hogwarts students doing their back-to-school shopping.

DESCRIPTION OF CARE OF MAGICAL CREATURES "CLASSROOM"

Care of Magical Creatures lessons typically take place outdoors near Hagrid's hut, a short walk away from the castle. Some lessons take place in the pumpkin patch, on the castle lawn or even in the Forbidden Forest. Two exciting lessons take place near the edge of the forest: one on unicorns and the other on hippogriffs, the latter of which the students encounter in a paddock.

In Harry's fifth year, students trek into the forest where they encounter the herd of Thestrals that lives at Hogwarts.

During inclement weather, Care of Magical Creatures lessons may be moved indoors. An unused classroom on the ground floor of the castle is used in such a case during the 1995–1996 school year.

REQUIRED INSTRUCTION AND HAGRID'S LESSON PLANS

While Hagrid's passion for the subject of Care of Magical Creatures is undeniable, his fondness for lethal animals can make his teaching approach seem questionable at times. He possesses immense knowledge about magical creatures, but it could be argued he does not adequately pass that information on to his students in a practical way.

As with every other Hogwarts class, students in Care of Magical Creatures must sit an O.W.L. examination in their fifth year, which covers a number of creatures. Ideally, students will spend their fourth and fifth years studying these creatures in preparation for the test and not rearing murderous Blast-Ended Skrewts, as Harry and his friends do. In Harry's fourth year, rather than learning about Knarls, Kneazles, Crups and Porlocks, students spend Care of Magical Creatures lessons trying to avoid injury at the hands of the Skrewts. Hagrid only moves on to teach them about Nifflers and unicorns after Rita Skeeter publishes an unflattering article about him and the Skrewts' questionable origins.

The monstrous, lobster-like creatures are a noticeable change from the previous year's (1993–1994) content, however, in which Harry's class endures multiple lessons on the profoundly boring Flobberworm. Hagrid opts for this mundane coursework after Draco Malfoy ignores his instructions on how to approach a hippogriff and is wounded by an alarmed Buckbeak. Draco's obstinacy aside, it's unclear whether hippogriffs are age-appropriate creatures for third-year students. Hagrid does have a tendency to introduce students to particularly dangerous animals earlier than other, more traditional Care of Magical Creatures instructors might, as evidenced by Professor Grubbly-Plank's lesson with Bowtruckles during Harry's fifth year.

During Harry's third year, Hagrid also teaches students about salamanders, yet his predecessor, Professor Kettleburn, doesn't seem to introduce salamanders until the fourth year. While Hermione finds Hagrid's lesson on Thestrals interesting, she notes a teacher like Grubbly-Plank probably wouldn't have introduced them until N.E.W.T. level.

While there is no reference to a set of educational standards for Care of Magical Creatures classes, by looking at how other teachers approach the subject, it's easy to see that Hagrid's lessons are considerably less formal, and he doesn't seem to have any qualms about having students encounter advanced creatures before they might be ready to handle them.

DIRECTORY OF KNOWN CREATURES USED IN COURSEWORK

BLAST-ENDED SKREWTS are a crossbreed between Fire Crabs and manticores. Hagrid breeds several hundred of the beasts prior to September 1994. When first hatched, Skrewts are pale, slimy, shell-less creatures that resemble lobsters whose legs stick out at odd angles. By the time they are several months old, Blast-Ended Skrewts grow to about 10 feet long and develop a shiny armor that proves impervious to most spells. Skrewts frequently shoot sparks from their back ends, which propels them forward several inches. The males have stingers and the females have suckers, which Hagrid believes are used to suck blood.

During the 1994–1995 school year, Hagrid tasks his fourth-year students with raising the Skrewts from hatchlings to adults. Since he doesn't know what the critters eat, his students must experiment by feeding them a variety of dishes including ant eggs, frog livers and grass snakes.

Although Blast-Ended Skrewts seem to be a violation of the Ban on Experimental Breeding, Hagrid is never charged with a crime in connection to breeding them.

BOWTRUCKLES are tree guardians that dwell in trees that provide wood of wandmaking quality. Professor Grubbly-Plank teaches a lesson on these creatures in Harry's fifth year. Described as looking like twigs and bark, Bowtruckles can be difficult to spot when in their natural habitat. Though they are peaceful creatures, Bowtruckles will gouge a person's eyes out if they feel their home tree is under attack. An offering of woodlice should placate Bowtruckles long enough for a witch or wizard to collect wand wood from their tree.

CRUPS are a wizard-created dog breed that resembles a Jack Russell terrier with a forked tail. Loyal to wizards, these magical canines are extremely ferocious toward Muggles; therefore, Crup owners must obtain a license from the Department for the Regulation and Control of Magical Creatures and pass a test to prove they can control the animal in Muggle-populated areas. Hogwarts students learn about Crups during the 1995–1996 school year in preparation for their O.W.L. examination.

FLOBBERWORMS are intensely dull creatures to learn about since they don't do much of anything. Described as brown, toothless worms, these creatures eat lettuce and cabbage. Students at Hogwarts learn about them in their third year. Flobberworm mucus is sometimes used to thicken potions.

HIPPOGRIFFS are half-horse, half-eagle creatures with the hindquarters of a horse and front legs that end in talons. Hippogriffs have the head of an eagle, with steel-colored beaks and orange eyes. A pair of powerful wings allows them to take flight.

Wizards keeping hippogriffs in areas populated by Muggles are required by law to cast Disillusionment Charms on them frequently in order to keep them hidden.

Hippogriffs are part of Hagrid's first lesson as a Hogwarts instructor. During this class, third-year students learn the proper etiquette needed to approach a hippogriff, which includes maintaining eye contact and bowing as a show of respect. If the hippogriff bows back, it is safe to approach.

KNARLS are almost identical to hedgehogs and often mistaken as such by Muggles. Aside from the magical properties of Knarl quills, a major difference between the two creatures can be found in how they react when given food by humans. A hedgehog will happily eat food left out for it, whereas a Knarl will view such offerings as an attempt to lure it into a trap or poison it. A Knarl suspecting such a trick will go on a rampage, destroying lawns and gardens in their wake. Knarls commonly appear on the O.W.L. examination, so fifth-year students study the creatures in preparation for the test.

KNEAZLES also frequently appear on O.W.L. examinations. These highly intelligent creatures are cat-like in appearance and often interbreed with domestic cats. Kneazle whiskers can be used as wand cores, but they are thought to make inferior wands compared to those with cores made of dragon heartstrings, unicorn hair or phoenix feathers.

NIFFLERS are mischievous creatures motivated by their love for all things shiny. Described as fluffy black creatures with long snouts, Nifflers are studied by fourth-year students.

During a lesson in the 1994–1995 school year, students are paired with a Niffler and take part in a treasure hunt: Hagrid offers a prize to the student whose Niffler digs up the most leprechaun gold, which he had buried in a patch of dirt.

PORLOCKS are studied by students in their fifth year at Hogwarts. Described as being about 2 feet tall with rough, shaggy hair, Porlocks walk on two cloven hooves and are known to guard horses. Porlocks are mistrustful of humans and usually hide at their approach. In the 14th century, the Wizards' Council classified Porlocks as beings due to the fact that they walk on two legs. However, they were later reclassified as beasts.

SALAMANDERS are covered in third- and fourth-year Care of Magical Creatures classes. Fire-dwelling salamanders are born in fires and live as long as the flames they were birthed in continue to burn. If fed pepper, salamanders can live outside of their flames for up to six hours.

THESTRALS are winged horses with skeletal bodies and reptilian features. They are invisible, appearing only to those who have witnessed death. This has earned them an undeserved reputation of being a bad omen. Thestrals have an excellent sense of direction and need only be told their destination to be able to fly straight there. Wizards keeping Thestrals in areas not protected from Muggles are required by law to cast Disillusionment Charms on them regularly.

During the 1995–1996 school year, Hagrid introduces fifth-year students to the herd of Thestrals living in the Forbidden Forest. More traditional teachers might have saved this particular lesson for students at the N.E.W.T. level.

UNICORNS are introduced to students in their fourth year. They are pure and gentle creatures that are easily recognized by their white coats and single horns. Unicorn foals are born with gold-colored coats that turn silver then white as they age. Hairs from a unicorn tail are used as wand cores, which are said to produce the most consistent magic. Unicorn horns are an ingredient in various potions.

CRUELTY-FREE TECHNIQUES FOR HANDLING MAGICAL CREATURES

With a little creativity and ingenuity, wizards can gently clear their space of garden and household pests with care for everyone involved.

Gnomes are a common garden pest found across Europe and North America. Wizarding gardens must be routinely de-gnomed, otherwise the gnome colonies will take over. The de-gnoming method recommended in *Fantastic Beasts and Where to Find Them* calls for swinging the gnome in circles to make it dizzy before dropping it over the garden fence. Disoriented, the gnome will wander off in a different direction and take a little longer to find its way back to the garden. The book's author, Newt Scamander, intended for his work to foster a better understanding of creatures and teach wizards how to care for them. By this logic, it would seem that the method recommended by Newt is considered cruelty-free and humane. If done as described in Newt's book, it certainly could be, but some wizards may take an exaggerated approach to these instructions. In 1992, Harry and the Weasley brothers turn de-gnoming the garden at the Burrow into a competition to see who can throw their gnome the farthest. Instead of lightly dropping the dizzied gnomes over the fence, the boys launch them through the air, which is far crueler than the de-gnoming procedure described in Newt's book.

According to *Fantastic Beasts*, **Jarveys** are a natural predator to gnomes. While setting a Jarvey loose on a garden full of gnomes is one way to deal with an infestation, most wizards nowadays find that method to be far too brutal. For a truly cruelty-free way to rid a garden of a gnome colony, lure them away by either installing a fake Jarvey to act as a scarecrow or setting up a decoy garden elsewhere in the vicinity.

Bowtruckles can also prove annoying to wizards hoping to collect wand wood. *Fantastic Beasts* recommends using woodlice or fairy eggs to placate Bowtruckles while removing wood from the trees they inhabit. However, these methods are only cruelty-free for the Bowtruckle. For a truly cruelty-free way to collect wand wood, one might consider encouraging the Bowtruckle and their branch (or group) to move to an alternative tree by briefly enchanting said tree to appear as though it's infested with woodlice. Grabbing Bowtruckles is not advised, especially when they're defending their tree, since forcibly moving them with one's hands could easily result in physical injury.

VARIOUS CREATURE AILMENTS AND TREATMENTS

Scale rot, which afflicts scaled creatures such as salamanders and dragons, causes the animal's scales to become flakey and dull or, at worst, slough off. In extreme cases, tail detachment can occur in salamanders. There is no single treatment for scale rot. For salamanders, rubbing chili powder on the affected areas until the rot heals is effective. In dragons, a solution consisting of white spirit, saltwater and tar should be administered.

Unwell creatures require specific diets to aid in healing as evidenced by the 1995–1996 O.W.L. exam, which involves selecting the appropriate food to give to a sick unicorn. It is unclear what the best approach to this situation is or what affliction would warrant a change in diet.

When Newt Scamander traveled the world in the 1920s, he brought along a case filled with a number of magical creatures. Over the course of his adventures, he administers eye drops to some of his mooncalves (whether it's because something is wrong with their eyes or if this is due to their eye size remains unclear). While on a mission, Newt removes a parasite from Yusuf Kama's eye, identifying it as one that is often carried by water dragons. It is not known how to treat the water dragon of the parasite, but the knowledge of a parasitic infection in one creature could imply that magical creatures, like most species, are susceptible to parasites. If these pests are similar to those of the Muggle world, they can be found both internally and externally, which would require different courses of treatment.

Charms

Charms are incredibly practical and are used on a daily basis by witches and wizards to perform small tasks and make life a little more convenient. Also referred to as enchantments, these spells can be defined as magic that can make objects or people behave in certain ways. They can also be used to add characteristics to objects and people, altering them to a degree without wholly transforming them into something else (i.e., transfiguration).

HISTORY OF CHARMS COURSE

Charms is one of the seven required core courses for Hogwarts students during the first five years of their education. After taking the O.W.L. exams, students can drop the class for their final two years in favor of subjects that better prepare them for their chosen career, though many popular careers require N.E.W.T.-level Charms instruction.

The course covers a variety of different charms for common uses. One of the most well-known charms is the Levitation Charm, which is taught to first-year students. These spells become progressively more difficult to perform—for example, moving from simply levitating an object to summoning it from hundreds of feet away—as students advance at Hogwarts. Some charms even require additional reading materials to prepare students for their lessons.

During their early years, students are taught to focus on the pronunciation of incantations and to memorize precise wand movements. As Professor Flitwick reminds students during the 1991–1992 school year, a simple mispronunciation could yield unexpected results, like ending up with a buffalo magically appearing on your chest.

All students take the O.W.L. for the course during their fifth year, which typically consists of two portions: written and practical. The written portion allows students to show their theoretical knowledge of the subject, like incantations and wand movements, whereas the practical section allows them to demonstrate their competency in casting charms.

As students move to N.E.W.T. level, they learn to cast nonverbal spells, which takes a significant amount of concentration and skill. Students are expected to cast spells nonverbally as often as possible from this point forward in Charms, Defense Against the Dark Arts and Transfiguration.

An "Outstanding" or "Exceeds Expectations" is needed on the Charms O.W.L. and N.E.W.T. exams to become an Auror or Healer. A grade of similar merit is probably needed for other career paths.

NOTABLE CHARMS PROFESSORS AND STUDENTS

Professor Filius Flitwick has taught Charms at Hogwarts since at least the time the Marauders attended the school. He is a well-accomplished Charms caster, which many believe has attributed to his success in dueling as rumored during Harry's second year. Given his chosen profession, he likely took Charms at an advanced level when he was a student at Hogwarts.

Hermione Granger is so well versed in Charms that she receives a stunning 112 percent on the final exam during her first year. It isn't clear how she obtains such a high mark, but considering her nature, she likely includes additional information or goes so far as to make edits to exam questions to add clarity. During a sixth-year class, Hermione is the only individual who successfully turns vinegar into wine. She also receives an "Outstanding" on the O.W.L. exam, continuing on to N.E.W.T. level. When Hermione returns to Hogwarts after Voldemort's demise, it's very likely that she lands high scores on her N.E.W.T. exam.

During Harry's sixth year, **Tom Marvolo Riddle** is described as having achieved high marks on every exam he took as a student, from which it can be inferred that he received high marks on the Charms O.W.L. and N.E.W.T. exams.

REQUIRED CHARMS TEXTBOOKS BY YEAR

The Standard Book of Spells, Grades 1 through 7, by Miranda Goshawk is a series used throughout a student's education at Hogwarts. Each grade corresponds to a different year at Hogwarts, meaning that by the end of their education, a student will have acquired a complete set of Goshawk's works. Goshawk, or her ancestor of the same name, previously wrote *The Book of Spells*, a clear and concise guide to spell-casting meant to replace the more complicated texts of the time. A copy of *The Book of Spells* is housed in the Restricted Section of the Hogwarts library. While there are similarities between the two texts, the *Standard Book of Spells* collection is better designed to accompany the Hogwarts Charms curriculum due to its book-per-year model. Each volume likely includes the charms covered during that year of coursework, meaning Grade 1 would include information on the Levitation Charm, while Grade 4 would detail the use of the Summoning Charm.

Quintessence: A Quest (author unknown) is used by students completing Charms at the N.E.W.T. level during the 1996–1997 school year. Students are required to have finished the book before the Christmas holiday. Harry turns to the book during his sixth year to avoid talking to Ron about Hermione's love life.

Three additional unnamed books are assigned to students during Harry's fourth year in preparation for a lesson on the Summoning Charm.

NOT REQUIRED BUT HELPFUL

Hermione consults **Achievements in Charming** by Sameera Hanifus during the 1995–1996 school year to study for the Charms O.W.L. exam.

Harry, Ron and Hermione use **An Anthology of Eighteenth-Century Charms** (author unknown) extensively during the 1994–1995 school year in an effort to help Harry prepare for the second task of the Triwizard Tournament, though they ultimately do not use any information from it. A copy is available in the library.

The trio also reviews *Olde and Forgotten Bewitchments and Charmes* (author unknown) in preparation for the Triwizard Tournament. It can be found in the library.

DESCRIPTION OF CHARMS CLASSROOM

During the 1990s, while Harry attends Hogwarts, the Charms classroom is located on the castle's third floor, and the corridor in which it is located is often referred to as the Charms corridor. This is not to be confused with Professor Flitwick's office, which is located on the seventh floor. The classroom has at least one window, which overlooks the entrance to Hogwarts. Professor Flitwick stands on a pile of books at the front of the classroom. During the Christmas season of Harry's third year, the professor decorates the space with fluttering fairies.

While the locations of the classroom and the professor's office are known, some speculation is needed regarding the materials and supplies present in the room. Like other classrooms, it's likely the room has rows of wooden desks or tables for students to sit at and practice their charm work in addition to a professor's desk. It's also probable that there is enough space to push the desks or tables together or apart, creating either larger desk spaces to work together or substantial open spaces to practice charms.

Students learn a variety of charms over the course of their education that require different materials. These items, such as feathers or cushions, are probably stored in the classroom as opposed to conjured when needed. Storage cabinets might line the walls of the room. Students also learn a variety of wand movements and incantations, which may be listed on large pieces of parchment around the classroom when each charm is covered. There may also be blackboards to write out incantations and wand or hand movements.

How Charms Differ From Curses and Hexes

The difference between a charm, jinx, hex and curse might not be readily apparent. Charms can mostly be classified as functional spells that witches and wizards use to navigate daily life, including the creation of Portkeys for traveling, making brooms fly and hiding the magical world from Muggle eyes. There are, however, other spells that possess the same characteristics as charms but are intended to cause discomfort, injury, pain and even death. These spells are typically referred to as jinxes, hexes and curses.

JINXES are spells that are used to create minor discomfort, like the Knockback Jinx. This spell is usually cast with the intention to knock a person or target backward and is popular in duels.

HEXES are spells that can cause mild suffering to their victims and can even be dangerous. Take the Hurling Hex, for example: Typically placed on brooms, it causes the broomstick to throw off its rider.

CURSES are spells cast with the intention to seriously harm, injure or even kill the target. Curses are usually hard to reverse and in some instances are irreversible. Examples include the three Unforgivable Curses, as well as the curse placed on Marvolo Gaunt's ring, an unknown lethal spell that afflicts Albus Dumbledore when he places the ring on his finger, injuring his hand and dramatically decreasing his life expectancy. Even though Dumbledore manages it with treatment from Severus Snape, the curse would have eventually killed him.

Charms on Objects vs. Charms on People

Witches and wizards place charms on objects with the goal of making the object behave a certain way or serve a particular purpose. Casting the Levitation Charm, for example, lifts an object into the air. The Summoning Charm brings objects to the caster, and the Unlocking Charm causes locked objects to unlock without the use of a key. During the 1991–1992 academic year, Professor Flitwick casts a charm on several keys so they can fly around a room. In some ways, charming objects endows them with almost lifelike properties.

Charms placed on people, on the other hand, likely require more skill and power to have the desired effect. Objects can't resist charms (unless they are bewitched to do so), whereas people have the ability to use a countercharm or a Shield Charm to protect them from the effects of a spell. Charms placed on people, especially those cast by younger witches and wizards, tend to wear off quickly while charms placed on objects tend to last longer.

THE DARK MAGIC HYPOTHESIS: IS A CURSE JUST A DARK MAGIC CHARM?

Curses can be defined as spells that are cast with the intent to seriously harm or kill the target. This can be done by casting a curse on an object, which in turn curses the person who touches it. It can also be cast on a person directly, with devastating effects.

But is a curse in its simplest form a Dark charm? It might be safe to say that charms form the basis for curses. Hexes and jinxes could likely be defined as charms that are darker than usual—they are annoying and sometimes humorous, and while they may cause the target some discomfort, they're not intended to achieve any Dark purpose. It is likely this branch of magic was first invented by someone manipulating the magic of some of the most powerful charms. If jinxes and hexes are slightly darker versions of typical charms, it could be argued that in creating curses, an individual simply took jinxes and hexes to the next level. So while a curse might not necessarily be defined as a Dark charm, charms likely serve as the basis on which curses were built in the first place.

THE USE OF WANDS IN CASTING CHARMS

Wands are vital tools when it comes to casting charms. A wand's primary purpose is to help witches and wizards focus their magic and then direct it at their target. Using a wand to cast a spell requires concentration and willpower, especially if the spell is advanced. For example, the Patronus Charm requires the caster to focus all their willpower on a happy memory, but this simple act necessitates profound focus when casting it in the presence of Dementors.

Wand movements are also essential when it comes to casting charms. Learning new spells requires students to memorize these gesticulations in order to perform them correctly. Some charms call for intricate wand flourishes, while simple waves or jabs suffice for others. With the Levitation Charm, the caster must "swish and flick" their wand to produce the correct results.

Wandless magic does exist, although it's not very common among wizards. Usually, the type of magic performed without a wand is unpredictable because the caster can't properly focus and direct their powers. Some wizards, like those attending the African school of magic Uagadou, are quite skilled at performing magic without wands. Creatures like house-elves and goblins, meanwhile, are also able to practice wandless magic with ease.

FAMOUS CHARMS USED BY HARRY AND HIS FRIENDS

Hundreds of charms exist in the magical world, but some are more popular than others when wizards find themselves facing an opponent.

THE TROLL IN THE BATHROOM VS. RON WEASLEY
- **Incantation** *Wingardium Leviosa*   **Name of Spell** Levitation Charm
  Purpose Causes an object to levitate
  Ron casts this charm in his first year while trying to save Hermione from the troll that Quirrell let into the castle. The spell lifts the troll's club into the air, and it ends up knocking the creature unconscious.

GILDEROY LOCKHART'S DUELING CLUB
- **Incantation** *Rictusempra*   **Name of Spell** Tickling Charm
  Purpose Causes the target to experience an uncontrollable tickling sensation

- **Incantation** *Tarantallegra*   **Name of Spell** Dancing Feet Spell
  Purpose Makes the target break out into an uncontrollable quickstep
  Harry casts the Tickling Charm on Draco Malfoy. Draco hits back with the Dancing Feet Charm.

BATTLING DEMENTORS
- **Incantation** *Expecto Patronum*   **Name of Spell** Patronus Charm
  Purpose To repel Dementors
  During the 1993-1994 academic year, Harry uses this spell during a Dementor attack in an attempt to save Sirius Black.

THE TRIWIZARD TOURNAMENT
General Spells Used Throughout the Tournament
- **Incantation** *Sonorus*   **Name of Spell** Amplifying Charm
  Purpose To amplify the target's voice when they need to speak to a large crowd
  The Amplifying Charm is used regularly when one of the teachers or organizers needs to address the crowd during a task.

First Task
- **Incantation** *Aguamenti*   **Name of Spell** Water-Making Spell
  Purpose Causes a clean jet of water to emerge from the tip of the caster's wand
  Fleur Delacour uses the Water-Making Spell to put out the fire on her robes during the first task.

- **Incantation** *Accio*   **Name of Spell** Summoning Charm
  Purpose To summon specific objects to the caster.
  Harry uses the Summoning Charm to summon his broomstick.

Second Task
- **Incantation** Unknown   **Name of Spell** Bubble-Head Charm
  Purpose Creates a bubble-like protection around the caster's head, providing them with oxygen while underwater
  Cedric Diggory and Fleur Delacour use the Bubble-Head Charm to breathe underwater.

Third Task
- **Incantation** *Periculum*   **Name of Spell** Red Sparks Charm
Purpose Shoots red sparks from the caster's wand

- **Incantation** *Riddikulus*   **Name of Spell** Boggart-Banishing Spell
Purpose Causes a boggart to assume a humorous form, counteracting its ability to terrify the caster

- **Incantation** *Point Me*   **Name of Spell** Four-Point Spell
Purpose Allows the caster to use their wand as a compass

- **Incantation** *Lumos*   **Name of Spell** Wand-Lighting Charm
Purpose Illuminates the tip of the caster's wand so they can see in the dark

- **Incantation** *Expelliarmus*   **Name of Spell** Disarming Charm
Purpose Causes whatever the target is holding to fly out of their hands.
  The Red Sparks Charm is used so teachers can easily locate students who run into trouble. Harry uses the rest of these charms while navigating the maze. He casts the Boggart-Banishing Spell when he realizes the Dementor in his midst is a boggart, employs the Four-Point Spell to help him find his way to the cup and uses the Wand-Lighting Charm to navigate through the dark. Harry eventually employs the Disarming Charm in order to free himself from an Acromantula's grasp. He uses it again while facing off against Voldemort in the graveyard after the Triwizard Cup (a Portkey in disguise) transports him there.

THE BATTLE OF THE DEPARTMENT OF MYSTERIES
- **Incantation** *Alohomora*   **Name of Spell** Unlocking Charm
Purpose Unlocks locked objects like doors and windows

- **Incantation** *Protego*   **Name of Spell** Shield Charm
Purpose Creates a shield that deflects spells from the caster

Hermione uses the Unlocking Charm in the Department of Mysteries to try to unlock one of the doors without success. Harry uses the Shield Charm to thwart the Death Eaters' attempts to get the prophecy.

HARRY POTTER VS. SEVERUS SNAPE
- **Incantation** *Incarcerous*   **Name of Spell** Binding Charm
  Purpose Causes thick ropes to attack and bind the target

- **Incantation** *Stupefy*   **Name of Spell** Stunning Spell
  Purpose To render the subject unconscious
  Harry attempts to use the Binding Charm and casts the Stunning Spell against Severus Snape in 1997 as Snape flees the castle after killing Albus Dumbledore.

THE BATTLE OF HOGWARTS
- **Incantation** *Piertotum Locomotor*   **Name of Spell** Variation of the Locomotion Charm
  Purpose Brings the Hogwarts statues to life

- **Incantation** *Protego Horribilis*   **Name of Spell** Stronger variation of the Shield Charm
  Purpose Creates a large protective shield to protect Hogwarts from Dark magic and invasion
  Professor McGonagall uses the Locomotion Charm to order the Hogwarts statues to protect the school when Voldemort's forces close in on the grounds.
  Professor Flitwick casts the powerful Shield Charm to help construct a protective barrier around the school in anticipation of the Death Eaters' arrival.

Defense Against the Dark Arts

Described as "many, varied, ever-changing, and eternal" by Severus Snape, the Dark Arts constitute the evil underbelly of all that is possible in the magical world. The Dark Arts comprise any magic or magical entity that can cause its intended target harm (such as robbing beings of their autonomy, e.g., forcing individuals to commit acts against their will), pain or death. These are the chief aims of the three Unforgivable Curses—the Cruciatus Curse, the Imperius Curse and the Killing Curse—the evilest magic wizards have at their disposal, and which all magic folk must learn to avoid. Performing any of the spells can earn the caster a life sentence in Azkaban. Defending oneself against the evils of the world isn't limited to spellwork alone, though, and students must prepare to encounter any number of creatures and cursed items.

HISTORY OF DEFENSE AGAINST THE DARK ARTS COURSE

As a school subject, Defense Against the Dark Arts centers on using magic for protection against Dark creatures as well as confronting adversaries, encompassing such topics as curses, hexes, jinxes and related disciplines (e.g., potion-making). Since dueling and the Dark Arts can be traced back to the earliest uses of magic, the subject has likely been a part of the Hogwarts curriculum since the school's inception. Due to his pure-blood supremacist beliefs, Salazar Slytherin disagreed with his cofounders about teaching students from non-magical backgrounds. As someone who actively practiced the Dark Arts, he created a subterranean chamber in Hogwarts in which to house a basilisk, a monster ordered by Slytherin to purge the school of Muggle-born students. It's safe to say this course has always had a fraught history at Hogwarts, most notably during Harry's years at the school.

VOLDEMORT'S DEFENSE AGAINST THE DARK ARTS JINX

There's much speculation surrounding the curse Voldemort placed on the Defense Against the Dark Arts position. It may have been a strategy to further his agendas; however, two other scenarios are possible. These three theories take into account what little factual information is known about the jinx as a foundation to speculate based on Voldemort's other exploits.

UNWITTING ANGER

When Tom Riddle was rejected from the position for the second time, he was already thoroughly obsessed with Dark magic. It is possible that, in his seething anger, the Dark wizard unwittingly cast a jinx on the position. As he was leaving the castle, Riddle may have thought something along the lines of, "If I can't have it, no one can," so strongly that his magic manifested that reality. Owing to Riddle's volatile emotions and inflated ego, this theory suggests that his magic could have interpreted his thoughts and emotions as intent and acted accordingly. This would be similar to how a young child's magic—inherent and spontaneous—makes its first appearance in a highly emotional situation.

PETTY SLIGHT

At this point in his life, Riddle is still relatively young. Although he was already far along the path of darkness, this jinx may have been the result of an immature adult acting on the feelings of having been scorned. This theory would dictate that the jinx came about purposely, but with a much more shortsighted goal of lashing out at Dumbledore for denying Riddle what he feels was promised to him.

GRAND PLAN

Of course, the argument could be made that this jinx was part of some "grand plan." Some find this unlikely because of the Dark wizard's track record of poor organization and failure when it comes to plans and schemes.

A core subject, Defense Against the Dark Arts is required for first-through fifth-year students. All students must take the Defense Against the Dark Arts O.W.L. examination, which includes a written test (e.g., identifying traits of werewolves) and a practical test, which requires students to perform counterjinxes and defensive spells (e.g., the Boggart-Banishing Spell). During the practical portion of his O.W.L. in 1996, Harry earns bonus points for successfully casting a corporeal Patronus Charm at the examiner's request.

Only students who achieve a score of either Exceeds Expectations or Outstanding for their O.W.L. may advance to N.E.W.T. level for this subject. Although Severus Snape restricts his N.E.W.T.-level Potions class to only those students with top marks, those with Exceeds Expectations are able to take Defense Against the Dark Arts in their sixth year when Snape takes over the subject in 1996.

In their sixth year, students are taught how to perform nonverbal spells and are expected to use that method of spellwork in their Defense Against the Dark Arts studies from that point forward.

The curriculum and required texts vary according to the teacher. Hoping to succeed retiring professor Galatea Merrythought, Tom Riddle applied for the teaching post twice: once shortly following his seventh year and again many years later after becoming more notorious for his dark dealings. After Headmaster Albus Dumbledore declined Riddle's second application, Riddle jinxed the teaching post; for various reasons, no single teacher has lasted in the position more than a year, a circumstance that only ends with Voldemort's demise in 1998.

Defense Against the Dark Arts lessons are generally balanced between theoretical knowledge and more practical demonstrations and activities. Depending on the teacher's preferred style, assessments can include essays, quizzes, written tests and practical exams.

NOTABLE PROFESSORS AND STUDENTS

Most of the following professors are brave enough to take on the cursed position during Harry's time at Hogwarts. The two notable exceptions—Professor Galatea Merrythought and Professor Albus Dumbledore—taught Defense Against the Dark Arts before Riddle placed a curse on the position.

- **Galatea Merrythought** – 1895–1945
- **Albus Dumbledore** – 1913, 1927
- **Quirinus Quirrell** – 1991–1992
- **Gilderoy Lockhart** – 1992–1993
- **Remus Lupin** – 1993–1994
- **Bartemius Crouch, Jr.**
  (disguised as Alastor "Mad-Eye" Moody) – 1994–1995
- **Dolores Umbridge** – 1995–1996
- **Severus Snape** – 1996–1997
- **Amycus Carrow** – 1997–1998

Harry receives an O (Outstanding) for his Defense Against the Dark Arts O.W.L. exam, which is hardly a surprise, given it's his favorite subject. He even manages to outperform **Hermione**, who receives an E (Exceeds Expectations). **Ron** also gets an O.W.L. in the subject. It can be deduced that **Fred and George Weasley** achieved the necessary O.W.L. grade in the subject since they were attending Professor Moody's classes during Harry's fourth year. Ron's brothers **Bill and Percy Weasley** both got 12 O.W.L.s in their fifth year, including Defense Against the Dark Arts.

REQUIRED DEFENSE AGAINST THE DARK ARTS TEXTBOOKS BY YEAR

Due to the high turnover rate for professors, required texts vary from year to year. Beyond the titles listed below, more books on the Dark Arts can be found in the Hogwarts library. Owing to their dark subject matter, some titles are kept locked in the Restricted Section and require special permission to access. It can be assumed that certain books detailing how to practice the Dark Arts, such as books on Horcruxes, may have been available in the Hogwarts library when Tom Riddle was a student.

Because the Defense Against the Dark Arts curriculum often overlaps with that of other subjects such as Charms and Potions, other required textbooks may be referenced while studying defensive magic, such as Miranda Goshawk's *Standard Book of Spells* series.

When Albus Dumbledore taught Defense Against the Dark Arts in the 1910s and 1920s, two of his assigned texts included **Defense Against the Dark Arts** and the fifth volume of **Advanced Defense Against the Dark Arts**, both authored by Galatea Merrythought. As of the 1991–1992 school year, all first-year Hogwarts students are assigned **The Dark Forces: A Guide to Self-Protection** by Quentin Trimble. This book may have been chosen by Quirinus Quirrell, although in any case, it still appears to be assigned or at least used by fourth-year students again in 1994. It covers information on Dark creature characteristics, such as werewolf bite treatment and defensive and offensive spell-casting. Trimble's book can be purchased at Flourish and Blotts in Diagon Alley.

During the 1992–1993 school year, the vain and self-absorbed Gilderoy Lockhart requires his students to purchase seven of his best-selling works:

- *Break with a Banshee*
- *Gadding with Ghouls*
- *Holidays with Hags*
- *Travels with Trolls*
- *Voyages with Vampires*
- *Wandering with Werewolves*
- *Year with the Yeti*

These titles are believed to chronicle Lockhart's epic feats during his international travels. However, it is later revealed that Lockhart is, in fact, a fraud who steals credit for better wizards' achievements after wiping their memories of the events. Lockhart's reasoning for claiming the credit for these acts is that the original witch or wizard who accomplished the feat was uninteresting or unappealing. Though the Dark creature at the center of each book was indeed defeated by a real witch or wizard, the books themselves are never commented on as being very helpful in teaching students the finer points of defensive magic.

During the 1995–1996 school year at Hogwarts, the Ministry-appointed professor Dolores Umbridge seeks a complete overhaul of the Defense Against the Dark Arts curriculum. This includes assigning the textbook *Defensive Magical Theory* by Wilbert Slinkhard to all students. Though the Ministry approves the book as a safe and age-appropriate alternative to previously assigned texts, students heavily criticize the text for its emphasis on theoretical knowledge and total lack of information regarding the use of defensive spells in real-world situations.

Confronting the Faceless (author unknown) is a textbook Severus Snape assigns N.E.W.T.-level Defense Against the Dark Arts students in 1996. It can be assumed that this book covers N.E.W.T.-level topics like Unforgivable Curses, Inferi and Dementors.

It is unclear which books, if any, are assigned by Death Eater Amycus Carrow when he instructs the class (simply "Dark Arts") during the 1997–1998 school year.

DESCRIPTION OF DEFENSE AGAINST THE DARK ARTS CLASSROOM

Though Defense Against the Dark Arts is taught by many different teachers over the years due to Tom Riddle's jinx, there are only two known classrooms dedicated to the subject. In 1992, Lockhart shepherds Harry through a side entrance into the castle before climbing one flight of stairs to his classroom, which would place the classroom on the first floor (above the ground floor). Sometime between Harry's second and sixth year, however, the location of these classes switches to the third floor. It's possible the third floor is the usual location and that Quirrell and Lockhart occupy a temporary or alternate classroom while the third floor is considered out-of-bounds during the year the Sorcerer's Stone is kept at Hogwarts.

In any case, the classroom is described as having desks for the students and teacher as well as windows that overlook the castle grounds. There is also an iron chandelier (from which Neville Longbottom dangles courtesy of Lockhart's escaped pixies), various cages or tanks containing whichever creatures the students may be studying and pictures lining the walls. In the 1992–1993 school year, these pictures depict Lockhart. When Snape takes over four years later, the walls are adorned with images of victims of Dark magic that illustrate such dangers as the Cruciatus Curse, the Dementor's Kiss and Inferi. The former Potions Master evokes his familiar gloomy dungeon environment by drawing the curtains over the windows so that the typically sunny room is lit only by candlelight.

Occasionally, Defense Against the Dark Arts classes and private lessons are given in other locations throughout the school. At least once, Remus Lupin brings his class of third-year Gryffindors to practice on a boggart trapped in the staffroom wardrobe. The staffroom is only a short walk away from Lupin's classroom. Three years later, when then Potions Master Severus Snape gives Harry private lessons in Occlumency, the meetings take place in Snape's dungeon office.

VARIOUS CURRICULA AND TEACHING METHODS

While most of the subjects Harry studies at Hogwarts have static professors and a linear curriculum, the jinx placed on the Defense Against the Dark Arts teaching post by Tom Riddle makes for a hodgepodge of topics and teaching methods. Some teachers come into the position from other subjects, such as Quirinus Quirrell and Severus Snape, who previously taught Muggle Studies and Potions, respectively. Other teachers come to the post from various backgrounds in the field, such as Remus Lupin's experience in the Order of the Phoenix or Alastor Moody's status as an accomplished Auror. Most teachers take up the role seemingly with the intention of lasting multiple years only to be thwarted in different ways by Riddle's jinx. Others, like Moody and Snape, are placed in the role with the understanding (whether public or private) that they will vacate the position after one year.

Some teachers are better received than others, but by the time Voldemort has returned to his body and Dolores Umbridge restricts the subject to basic theory, many students decide to take their education into their own hands, forming Dumbledore's Army to study practical defensive magic in secret.

Even though the subject is supposed to be centered on defending against the Dark Arts, it appears the teaching position attracts Dark witches and wizards. In fact, several Death Eaters or others who practice Dark magic have applied for or been placed in the role.

Tom Riddle applied twice. He was first turned down by Headmaster Armando Dippet, whose reasoning was that the recent Hogwarts graduate did not have the requisite experience. Riddle's reasons for applying at this point were supposedly (according to Dumbledore) because he regarded the school as home, he wanted to discover more of the castle's ancient mysteries, and he desired the ability to wield great influence over young witches and wizards and recruit them to his cause. When Riddle applied again several years later, the sitting headmaster, Albus Dumbledore, gave a second refusal. Dumbledore maintained Riddle did not actually want to be appointed in the role, but that he likely only returned to the castle to leave behind Ravenclaw's diadem, which was now also a Horcrux. It was from this point onward that the jinx was placed, and no professor would last more than a year in the role until after Riddle's death in 1998.

One Dark Arts practitioner who succeeds in landing the role of Defense Against the Dark Arts professor during the 1991–1992 academic year is **Quirinus Quirrell**, who devotes himself to Voldemort shortly before Harry's arrival at Hogwarts. With a disembodied Voldemort secretly attached to the back of his head, Quirrell does his master's bidding while masquerading as a timid, stuttering teacher. His ruse is successful because most students regard him as a thoroughly unthreatening fool, but he ultimately shows himself to be evil by attempting to murder 11-year-old Harry. Despite (or perhaps because of) his allegiance to Voldemort, Quirrell's teaching style of focusing on theoretical knowledge is hailed by Umbridge years later.

Gilderoy Lockhart is a highly anticipated addition to the staff at Hogwarts the following year, but he is quickly revealed to be a terrible teacher due to the lack of actual instruction in class. Rather than focus on defense content, the self-centered charlatan gives quizzes about his own likes and dislikes, and after one fiasco involving the escape of many Cornish pixies, his classes are relegated to theatrics and reminiscing about his fake experiences with Dark creatures. Most promising, perhaps, is his Dueling Club (through which the assisting teacher, Severus Snape, introduces Harry to what would become the latter's signature spell: the Disarming Charm), but Lockhart is of little aid during the club's first and only meeting. He's even less useful in dealing with the opening of the Chamber of Secrets.

Remus Lupin is regarded by many as a superb Defense Against the Dark Arts teacher, even after he is outed as a werewolf and sacked at the end of the 1993–1994 school year. Similar to Albus Dumbledore, who held the position almost a century earlier, Lupin is well-liked by most students, maintaining a good rapport with them and encouraging them to practice during class. In the first lesson of the school year, he even allows third years to jump into their practical applications by facing off against a real boggart. He sets a unique style of exam in the format of an obstacle course, in which students can work through various challenges with Dark creatures in a real-world setting. A modest professor, he initially hesitates to teach Harry the Patronus Charm, saying he is not the most experienced at fighting Dementors. His work pays off later that year when Harry saves Sirius Black's life by casting an exceptionally strong Patronus during a Dementor attack.

Some Slytherin students openly criticize Lupin's shabby appearance, and Umbridge regards him as a dangerous half-breed. Still, most students remember Lupin as the best Defense Against the Dark Arts teacher they ever had. When Harry leads Dumbledore's Army, his practical and inspiring teaching style draws much from Lupin's approach.

Barty Crouch, Jr., uses Polyjuice Potion to impersonate Alastor "Mad-Eye" Moody for the duration of the 1994–1995 school year. The Azkaban escapee is the second of Voldemort's followers to land the job. In the guise of Moody, Crouch is viewed as harsh by students who feel he takes his work too far, notably when he demonstrates illegal Unforgivable Curses in class for fourth years (the topic is usually reserved for N.E.W.T. level). On the whole, students are generally impressed by "Moody," given his extensive experience in the field and pragmatic approach. Crouch even performs the Imperius Curse on students to give them the chance to practice defending themselves against it. Despite the fact that he is an escaped Death Eater actively cursing Harry and his classmates, Crouch ultimately ensures his students are adequately prepared to face real-life encounters with Dark forces. Because his farce is so believable, Crouch numbers among Harry's better teachers, even though he, too, attempts to kill the Boy Who Lived by year's end.

Dolores Umbridge, Senior Undersecretary to Minister of Magic Cornelius Fudge, succeeds Crouch as Defense Against the Dark Arts professor. Her installment is part of a larger effort by the Ministry of Magic to gain control of the curriculum and prevent Dumbledore from spreading the news about Voldemort's return. One can hardly call what Umbridge does teaching, since her classes consist only of directing students to read about defensive theory in silence. Though she isn't a Death Eater or Voldemort devotee like two of her predecessors, Umbridge arguably does the most damage during her time at Hogwarts by keeping her students in the dark, especially once she is named Hogwarts High Inquisitor and headmistress. She meets opposition from staff and students alike with her theory-based classes and general obstruction, getting rid of staff and banning anything she feels poses a threat to herself or to the ministry's rule. Worst of all, she resorts to torturing students with a scalpel-like magic quill that scars Harry's hands while he uses it to write lines in detention. She even attempts to cast the Cruciatus Curse on Harry when he refuses to answer her questions after breaking into her office.

Severus Snape, who applies time and time again for the role of Defense Against the Dark Arts professor, is repeatedly denied the position by Dumbledore, who fears the role will bring out the worst in the former Death Eater. It is likely Dumbledore also wishes to protect Snape from the effects of Riddle's jinx on the job. When Dumbledore recognizes he will die after having touched a cursed object, the headmaster relents and agrees to give Snape his dream appointment, knowing full well that Snape would need to kill him before the end of the year as part of their plan to protect Harry. As Defense Against the Dark Arts professor, Snape places an emphasis on understanding and respecting the Dark Arts. Harry interprets Snape's passionate lectures as indicative of a fondness for the Dark Arts, but Hermione points out that Snape and Harry speak similarly about the subject; both student and teacher emphasize how one must be ready for anything with a sharp mind and quick reflexes.

Amycus Carrow takes over the class during the 1997–1998 school year after Death Eaters invade Hogwarts. As a follower of Voldemort, he retools its content into simply the Dark Arts. As Death Eaters, Carrow and his sister, Alecto, have students perform Dark magic on each other, including the Cruciatus Curse, as a form of cruel and unusual punishment. Carrow does not get along with fellow teachers like Minerva McGonagall who remain in their posts to protect students from this type of abuse.

After the Battle of Hogwarts, the removal of the Carrows and Voldemort's death, Riddle's jinx is lifted and the subject can once again be taught by a single teacher over the course of many years.

DIRECTORY OF KNOWN CREATURES USED IN DEFENSE AGAINST THE DARK ARTS COUSEWORK

To round out the curriculum in Defense Against the Dark Arts, students are taught about various Dark creatures.

BANSHEES are native to Ireland and are malevolent beings that take the form of women. Their unpleasant cries are said to herald death.

BOGGARTS are technically "non-beings" but are typically categorized as creatures that shape-shift into an observer's worst fear.

CORNISH PIXIES are amall, bright blue and fond of mischief. These known tricksters have incredibly shrill voices, adding to the sense of chaos that surrounds their antics.

GHOULS are slimy, buck-toothed magical beasts that tend to live in the attics or barns of wizarding dwellings. While relatively harmless, they can make a lot of noise.

GRINDYLOWS are small, horned water demons native to the United Kingdom. They are aggressive and can be found at the bottom of lakes.

HAGS are vicious beings who eat children. They look like witches with many warts and may have magical abilities similar to those of trolls.

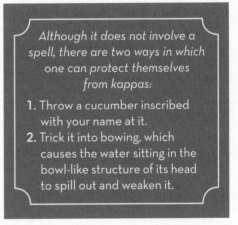

Although it does not involve a spell, there are two ways in which one can protect themselves from kappas:

1. Throw a cucumber inscribed with your name at it.
2. Trick it into bowing, which causes the water sitting in the bowl-like structure of its head to spill out and weaken it.

HINKYPUNKS appear as wispy smoke. These small, one-legged beasts are known for luring travelers off their path and into bogs.

KAPPAS are japanese water demons that look like scaly monkies with webbed hands. They are known to strangle humans and feed on their blood.

RED CAPS are small, dwarf-like beasts that live wherever human blood has been spilled. They are fond of castle dungeons and the potholes of old battlefields.

TROLLS are magical beasts of immense strength and huge stature. Violent by nature, they enjoy eating human flesh. Except for security trolls, trolls do not mingle with wizards or Muggles.

VAMPIRES sustain themselves by drinking blood. These Dark beings are largely feared by wizards and monitered by the Ministry.

WEREWOLVES transform from regular wizards into uncontrollable, deadly wolf-like creatures as the full moon rises. However, if they take the Wolfsbane Potion beforehand, they can retain their human mind.

YETIS are magical humanoid beasts native to Tibet that can grow up to 15 feet tall. They will attack and eat anything they find.

ZOMBIES are undead corpses known for their gray skin and rotten smell that are native to the Southern United States. Unlike Inferi, which are dead bodies reanimated by Dark magic, zombies are considered creatures as opposed to people.

IDENTIFYING CURSED ITEMS

It is unknown what methods determine whether or not an item is cursed, but one common characteristic appears to be that such items possess a semblance of sentience. At number twelve, Grimmauld Place, several items are "reluctant" to leave their shelves. While it is unknown whether or not all of these items are cursed, this implies a degree of malevolence. Horcruxes, one of the most evil forms of cursed objects, display this same characteristic in a more literal way: Tom Riddle's diary and Slytherin's locket actively attempt to kill anyone who tries to destroy them.

As demonstrated when Lily Potter died for her son, Harry, sacrificial love provides powerful protection against the Killing Curse.

KNOWN SPELLS AGAINST DARK MAGIC

Protection from Dark magic may not be as important to the average wizard as it is to Harry, but danger finds its way into even the quietest of lives.

Boggart-Banishing Spell (*Riddikulus*) This forces the boggart to assume an amusing form so that it can be banished with laughter.

Counterjinx for the Dangling Jinx (*Liberacorpus*) This counterjinx will lower someone down if they have been made the levitating target of the Dangling Jinx.

General Countercharm (*Surgito*) A countercharm that can remove enchantments

General Counterspell (*Finite Incantatem*) This counterspell can stop the effects of some Dark magic.

Hex Deflection Spell (*Salvio Hexia*) This enchantment deflects hexes from their intended target.

Impediment Jinx (*Impedimenta*) This jinx can help slow down an attacker.

Knockback Jinx *(Flipendo)* This jinx knocks the target backward and can be used to defend oneself in a duel.

Pixie-Repelling Charm *(Peskipiksi Pesternomi)* A charm meant to capture or repel pixies, likely fabricated by Gilderoy Lockhart

Reviving Spell *(Rennervate)* This charm awakens an unconscious individual and works as a countercharm to the Stunning Spell.

Revulsion Jinx *(Relashio)* This jinx can be used to escape the grip of a grindylow by blasting streams of boiling water at it.

Shield Charm *(Protego)* This charm protects the caster with an invisible shield. Both spells and physical bodies are blocked with this charm.

EFFECT OF WORLD EVENTS ON DEFENSE AGAINST THE DARK ARTS

Although Hogwarts is physically tucked away from the rest of the world, it remains at the center of many aspects of wizarding society. The school's curriculum is influenced (even if indirectly) not just by the professors but also by the school governors and—to an extent—the Ministry of Magic. Current events within the wizarding community influence the public's discomfort with the Dark Arts, which then affects the education of young wizards.

Defense Against the Dark Arts may have been intended to teach young wizards about how to manage everyday Dark magic like ghouls in their attic or grindylows in their pond. However, the rise and fall of fascist leaders like Gellert Grindelwald and Voldemort, who prove willing to use Dark magic to achieve their aims, highlight this subject as a matter of life and death. During periods of strife, war and danger, Hogwarts classes are taught with an aggressive focus on practical assignments. During periods of peace, order and growth, classes tend to fall into a lull of theoretical focus.

Divination

D ivination is the process of foreseeing future events, often by looking for signs through physical means (e.g., reading tea leaves, palmistry, crystal gazing, dream interpretation, astrology, fire-omens). Some rare wizards possess the innate gift of unconsciously channeling prophecies via their Inner Eye. Such individuals are known as Seers. It should be noted that not all wizards embrace this field of study due to its high margin of error; some are more vocal about it than others.

HISTORY OF DIVINATION COURSE

Divination is an ancient kind of magic, practiced in many forms. Divination tools such as crystal balls are known to have been used by wizards from at least the 1920s into the 1990s. In the 1920s, the Dark wizard Gellert Grindelwald uses an unknown skull-shaped device to blow smoke, in which visions of the future can be seen.

The Ministry of Magic keeps a record of prophecies made by Seers in a space known as the Hall of Prophecy, which houses shelves of glass orbs containing predictions. In 1996, many of these prophecies are destroyed when Harry and his friends face off against Death Eaters during the Battle of the Department of Mysteries. Orbs aside, records of prophecies can also be recorded and published in book form.

There is an ancient wizarding practice that entails parents consulting a Naming Seer in order to choose a fitting name for their child. This tradition has fallen out of favor, however, as most parents are loath to hear negative predictions or prophecies of impending doom relating to their offspring.

Divination is an elective course offered to students in their third year of study. It is unknown how long the subject has been part of the Hogwarts curriculum.

Around 1980, Headmaster Albus Dumbledore considered discontinuing the teaching of the subject at Hogwarts. Before he could scrub it from the school's course offerings, though, he received a job application from Sybill Trelawney, a descendant of famed Seer Cassandra Trelawney. Impressed by her lineage, Dumbledore thought he owed Trelawney a chance to interview for the post of Divination professor. During their interview at the Hog's Head Inn, Trelawney went into a trance and made the prophecy that would prompt Voldemort to attempt to kill Harry Potter. Dumbledore hired Trelawney not only because she had demonstrated her abilities as a true Seer but also to protect her from Voldemort. Without knowing it, Trelawney had saved Divination from becoming a thing of the past at Hogwarts.

In the 1990s, when Headmistress Dolores Umbridge fires Trelawney from her post, Dumbledore arranges for the centaur known as Firenze to teach the subject. Centaurs are known to practice divination, and while Firenze doesn't shy away from imparting his methods to the class, he maintains that the process of determining the meanings of various signs can take upward of 10 years to complete.

Just like other Hogwarts classes, there is an O.W.L. examination in Divination. However, Professor Trelawney takes the stance that a passing grade on the exam is not needed to continue to develop one's Inner Eye.

Throughout Harry's time at Hogwarts, he and Ron have very little good to say about their Divination studies. While their disdain for the subject may stem from their lack of skill and feelings of inadequacy at predicting the future, divination is often scoffed at and looked down upon by many in the wizarding community due to its vague nature and imprecise methods. It can be hard to trust in something that is often wrong, can be easily misinterpreted, or—as is the case with Seers—can only be done by a handful of wizards born with special gifts.

Hermione considers it a "woolly" subject, and McGonagall calls it an imprecise branch of magic, even going so far as to imply Trelawney is a fraud. Despite these opinions, it is clear there are true practitioners of the art of divination, as evidenced by the orbs lining the shelves in the Hall of Prophecy at the Ministry of Magic.

Unlike many other esteemed wizards, Dumbledore appears to take divination very seriously. When Sybill Trelawney predicts the fall of

Voldemort, Dumbledore deduces that this prophecy is authentic, despite ample evidence pointing to Trelawney exaggerating or fabricating her abilities.

NOTABLE DIVINATION PROFESSORS AND STUDENTS

Professor Sybill Trelawney began teaching at Hogwarts in 1980. The great-great-granddaughter of **Cassandra Trelawney**, a gifted and respected Seer, Sybill inherited Cassandra's gift. She makes at least two prophecies about Lord Voldemort that ultimately come true: the prophecy that marked Harry Potter as "the Chosen One," which caused Voldemort to attempt to kill him as a baby, and the prediction that Voldemort would rise again to power after more than a decade of hiding in the shadows.

In the 1995–1996 school year, **Dolores Umbridge**, acting as the Hogwarts High Inquisitor, places Trelawney (whom she's deemed woefully inadequate as a professor) on probation and ultimately fires her. Rather than deliver the news in private, however, the ever-sadistic Umbridge takes things a step further by attempting to evict Trelawney from the castle in full view of students and staff. To Trelawney's relief, Dumbledore steps in and forbids Umbridge from banishing the professor from Hogwarts.

Though Trelawney is still allowed to stay at the castle, she is not permitted to resume teaching, forcing Dumbledore to hire a new Divination professor. **Firenze**, a centaur from the Forbidden Forest, accepts the job (though at the cost of being banished and nearly killed by his enraged herd for agreeing to teach humans). Firenze leads the class for the remainder of the school year in Trelawney's absence.

During the 1996–1997 school year, following Umbridge's removal from Hogwarts, Trelawney returns to her post to co-teach along with Firenze. Much as Dumbledore had kept Trelawney at Hogwarts for protection from Voldemort, he offers Firenze the chance to live in safety at the school due to his status as a pariah.

REQUIRED DIVINATION TEXTBOOKS BY YEAR

Unfogging the Future by Cassandra Vablatsky is required reading for Divination students beginning in their third year. The book can be purchased at Flourish and Blotts in Diagon Alley and includes information on crystal balls, palmistry and tessomancy (the art of reading tea leaves).

Pages five and six of *Unfogging the Future* hold information about interpreting tea leaves. In 1993, the third-year Divination class consults these pages to determine the meanings of various symbols found in the dregs of a cup of tea. According to the book, a cross signifies trials and suffering, the sun equates to happiness and an acorn predicts sudden riches. In 1994, Neville Longbottom consults the book for some last-minute studying on crystal gazing while waiting to take the end-of-year Divination exam.

The Dream Oracle by Inigo Imago is a book used by fifth-year Divination students at Hogwarts. In 1995, students enter the Divination classroom to find copies of the book have been placed on their desks. Rather than including it on a list of items for students to purchase prior to the start of term, Trelawney provides each student with a copy. These books remain in the room and are only used during class time.

This title is a guide for interpreting dreams and their meanings. The interpretation method requires adding the date the dream took place, the age of the dreamer and the number of letters in the dream's subject.

During the 1995–1996 school year, students are in the middle of consulting *The Dream Oracle* when Dolores Umbridge arrives to conduct an observation of Trelawney's class. After receiving the results of her inspection, the professor is so visibly rattled and angry that she throws a copy of *The Dream Oracle* at Seamus Finnigan and shoves one at Neville so hard he falls out of his seat.

DESCRIPTION OF DIVINATION CLASSROOM

The Divination classroom is located in the North Tower. It's a long trek from the Great Hall; to get there, one must climb seven staircases and traverse a long corridor before climbing a ladder that leads to a circular trapdoor in the ceiling.

This circular, windowed room is described as a cross between someone's attic and an old tea shop, with at least 20 round tables scattered throughout, surrounded by chintz armchairs and poufs. Red scarves are draped over the lamps, bathing the room in a red glow. The fireplace is often lit, even in the warmer months; it emits a perfumed scent and fills the room with stifling heat. In 1995, Harry claims a chintz armchair due to its proximity to a window, which he cracks open to try to feel a breeze. Supplies needed for Divination lessons can be found on shelves lining the walls, including candle stubs, crystal balls, feathers, packs of tattered playing cards and plenty of teacups.

Sybill Trelawney teaches in the North Tower classroom, but when Firenze joins the staff, he requires a ground-floor classroom, as the staircases and a ladder would prove difficult for a centaur to access. Firenze's Divination lessons are held in classroom 11, which is located on the ground floor of the castle, off of the corridor leading to the Entrance Hall. Prior to Firenze's employment, classroom 11 was rarely used and resembled a storeroom. However, during the 1995–1996 school year, the room is enchanted to imitate Firenze's home in the Forbidden Forest. The classroom floor is covered in moss, out of which trees grow, their branches covering the ceiling and windows so that the light filtering through is dappled green, much like the sun shining through a forest. Students sit on the ground rather than at desks, with their backs propped against boulders and tree stumps.

ORACLES AND SEERS THROUGHOUT WIZARDING HISTORY

TYCHO DODONUS was a wizard who made a series of prophecies, poetic in nature, that he compiled and published as *The Predictions of Tycho Dodonus* sometime prior to 1927.

GELLERT GRINDELWALD, the Dark wizard known for his plan of wizarding domination over Muggles, was also a Seer. In the 1920s, he used his visions of a second World War to his advantage to bring more followers to his side. His abilities also led him to New York, where he knew there was a child who held immense power.

CASSANDRA TRELAWNEY, the great-great-grandmother of Sybill Trelawney, is described as a gifted Seer who was well respected in her time. Her reputation is what prompted Dumbledore to agree to a job interview with Sybill when the latter sought employment at Hogwarts.

SYBILL TRELAWNEY teaches Divination at Hogwarts. She made the prediction that sent Voldemort after the Potter family, murdering Lily and James and marking Harry with a lightning-shaped scar.

TRELAWNEY'S PROPHECIES

In 1980, Sybill Trelawney made the prophecy that sent Voldemort after the Potters. She predicted a child born in the seventh month to parents who had defied Voldemort three times would have the power to vanquish him. Severus Snape, then a Death Eater, overheard this portion of the prophecy before he was caught eavesdropping outside the door. He relayed what he heard to Voldemort without realizing he had missed a crucial part of the prophecy: The child would have power that Voldemort did not, and by going after him, Voldemort would mark that individual as an equal. Most of all, as Harry crucially comes to find out, neither he nor the Dark wizard "can live while the other survives."

Trelawney delivered the prophecy while in a trance, with no memory of what she said after the fact. In June 1994, she enters that trance-like state again and predicts a servant of Voldemort will return to him after being "chained these twelve years" and help him rise to power once again. Soon enough, Peter Pettigrew escapes and returns to Voldemort after living for 12 years as the Weasley family rat, Scabbers. With Pettigrew's assistance, Voldemort regains his body the following summer.

In contrast to these prophecies, Trelawney also makes other predictions while not under a trance, which are often far more vague. During the first Divination class of the 1993–1994 school year, Trelawney issues a series of predictions involving her students, some of which appear to be nonsense: She implies Neville Longbottom's grandmother is ill (when, in fact, Augusta Longbottom appears to be in good health), that Neville will be late to class and that he'll break a teacup. While he does indeed shatter a teacup, these last two predictions could be considered nothing more than astute observations of Neville's general nature.

She doesn't end with Neville: Trelawney also tells Lavender Brown the thing she is "dreading" will occur on October 16. On that date, to Lavender's horror, she receives a letter from home that her rabbit, Binky, has died. As Hermione points out, however, Binky was a young rabbit, meaning Lavender wouldn't have been actively anticipating his demise, and he must have died prior to the 16th to allow time for the letter to be delivered.

While these predictions don't appear to be accurate, others from this same lesson come true in one way or another. Trelawney predicts that around Easter "one of our number will leave us forever," only for Hermione to storm out of Divination class and drop the course that spring.

Trelawney constantly makes predictions about her students, but Harry in particular—the Boy Who Lived—is a favorite subject. While teaching students about astrology, she deduces Harry must have been born under Saturn, which would have placed his birthday in mid-winter. Harry was in fact born in July, but Voldemort, his archenemy, was born in December, and it's possible she senses the fragment of Voldemort's soul that resides within Harry during this time. Trelawney foresees death for Harry at nearly every opportunity: She observes the Grim, a death omen in the shape of a dog, in the dregs at the bottom of his teacup. The shape of a black dog could refer to Sirius Black's Animagus form, but as Harry discovers during the Battle of Hogwarts in 1998, her grim predictions are not so ridiculous after all—when Harry allows himself to be struck by Voldemort's Killing Curse during the Battle of Hogwarts, he briefly enters limbo.

It doesn't take a Seer to predict violence lies in Harry's future, though—the centaurs in the Forbidden Forest also grasp that he is destined to confront Voldemort. In 1992, Firenze rescues Harry from

Voldemort while the latter laps up unicorn blood in the Forbidden Forest. His fellow centaurs believe that in doing so, Firenze is going "against the heavens" and interfering with what has been foretold. The centaurs also note that the planet Mars (named for the Roman god of war) shines brightly that night. By ingesting unicorn blood, Voldemort is getting closer to his goal of regaining a body, which means it won't be long until the magical community is plunged into a war for the ages.

THE GRIM

A large black dog known as "the Grim" is likely more of an urban legend than a true part of divination. Wizards believe seeing the creature means death is in one's very near future. Ron claims his Uncle Bilius died 24 hours after seeing the Grim. After leaving number four, Privet Drive prior to the start of the 1993 school year, Harry is spooked by what looks like a large black dog (later revealed to be Sirius in Animagus form). That same year, Trelawney claims to see the Grim in Harry's tea leaves during Divination class and Harry spots the Grim on a book cover at Flourish and Blotts.

FORMS OF DIVINATION

There's no one-size-fits-all method when it comes to unfogging the future:

ASTROLOGY is crucial to the type of divination practiced by centaurs. It is also used by wizards to foresee the future. For more information, see pg. 66.

AUGURY (Bird Entrail Reading) is the act of examining bird entrails to foretell events. In Cassandra Vablatsky's book *Unfogging the Future*, it's considered a classic method of fortune-telling.

CARTOMANCY (Card Reading) involves the use of playing cards, such as tarot cards, to foresee the future.

CHIROMANCY (Palmistry) entails interpreting certain details of a person's palm as a means to gain insight into that person's future.

CRYSTAL BALLS are orbs in which those who practice divination may be able to see objects, shapes or scenes (although it is unknown exactly what) that they can interpret.

DREAM INTERPRETATION entails analyzing actions and symbols within dreams, which can carry great weight when it comes to predicting events.

OVOMANCY (Egg Yolk Reading) is divination performed by cracking open eggs and observing how the yolks fall.

PYROMANCY (Fire Omens Symbols) involves reading shapes in a fire. Centaurs sometimes employ this method to gain more clarity from their astrological interpretations.

THE INNER EYE

Seers experience the gift of prophecy and are known to have the "Inner Eye." Little is known about why someone might possess the Inner Eye or the degree with which they can use it. Trelawney, for example, possesses the Inner Eye but only makes two real prophecies.

TASSEOGRAPHY (Tea Leaf Reading) is a process that entails pouring loose leaf tea into a cup, drinking it until only the dregs remain, swirling the cup three times with the left hand and turning the cup over to drain before reading the leaves.

INTERPRETING SIGNS

Some forms of divination provide specific static images for interpretation, such as cartomancy (card reading) and tasseography (tea leaf reading).

CARTOMANCY (According to Trelawney)
- **Two of Spades** conflict
- **Seven of Spades** an ill omen
- **Ten of Spades** violence
- **Knave of Spades** as the professor puts it, "A dark young man, possibly troubled, one who dislikes the questioner..."
- **Lightning-Struck Tower** *(The Tower; 16th card in the Major Arcana of the Tarot)* abrupt or violent change

TASSEOGRAPHY
- **Acorn** unexpected gold
- **Club** an attack
- **Cross** trials and suffering
- **Falcon** a deadly enemy
- **The Grim** omen of death
- **Sun** great happiness

Other types of divination provide less concrete images to interpret. For example, dreams not only vary from person to person but are also difficult to recall in exact and perfect detail, making it highly difficult to create a uniform guideline for how to interpret imagery. In a similar vein, interpreting fire omens is problematic due to the ever-changing nature of the flame and fume.

ASTROLOGY AND DIVINATION

Star charts are used not only to study celestial objects but also for divination purposes. A map of the sky from the exact moment of an individual's birth can be analyzed to interpret aspects of their future. For more on star charts, see pg. 67.

CENTAURS AND DIVINATION

Centaurs study the planetary movements in great detail over centuries, using the information they glean in their divination to understand what's happening in the world around them. They claim that the knowledge they gain from these practices is "impersonal and impartial" and keep their findings private.

Because their methods rely on planetary movements, insight into the future is rarely immediate. For example, Mars shining brightly above could indicate that a war will begin "soon." To determine a more accurate time frame than "soon," centaurs may burn certain herbs and leaves to observe fumes and flames.

When the centaur Firenze takes a teaching position at Hogwarts, he remains unconcerned when his students cannot see symbols or shapes in the flames or fumes. According to centaurs, humans are rarely good at this form of divination and it often takes many years to become competent. Firenze also notes that the signs can be read incorrectly, making it "foolish" to place too much faith in them.

Herbology

The mystical and mundane plants of the magical world, as well as their uses and practical applications, offer endless opportunities for study. Herbology provides students with the knowledge to seamlessly interact with the flora around them, from crafting plant-based potions to fending off vines inclined to strangle unsuspecting passersby.

HISTORY OF HERBOLOGY COURSE

Herbology is an ancient branch of magic that is as complex and varied as nature itself. The origins of its study are not well documented, but two wizards are frequently noted for their contributions to the field: Zygmunt Budge, who studied hundreds of secret plants to discover their properties, and Phyllida Spore, author of *One Thousand Magical Herbs and Fungi*. Spore's book is so influential, it is still assigned as a textbook at Hogwarts in the 1990s.

NOTABLE HERBOLOGY PROFESSORS AND STUDENTS

Professor Herbert Beery taught Herbology at Hogwarts under Headmaster Armando Dippet but left to pursue his passion for theater.

During Harry's years at Hogwarts, **Pomona Sprout** teaches the subject and serves as head of Hufflepuff House. She is known for her incredible herbology talent and teaching ability. She retires sometime by 2017 when she is succeeded by **Neville Longbottom**, who excelled at the subject during his time at the school.

REQUIRED HERBOLOGY TEXTBOOKS BY YEAR

One Thousand Magical Herbs and Fungi by Phyllida Spore is an essential textbook for all Herbology students at Hogwarts. Although little is known about Spore, her knowledge of magical flora is frequently referenced and highly trusted. First-year students are required to purchase the textbook before start-of-term, and it continues to serve them throughout their education.

During Harry Potter's time at Hogwarts, *One Thousand Magical Herbs and Fungi* is referenced by students in their first, fourth, fifth and sixth years. Second-, third- and seventh-year students also likely use it. Interestingly, Spore's book doubles as a useful guide for potioneers. Its pages outline the uses of magical plants and animal byproducts, with one entry describing Flobberworm mucus as a "popular potion thickener."

NOT REQUIRED BUT HELPFUL

Only two other books on herbology are mentioned during Harry's time at Hogwarts. During their fourth year, Neville Longbottom is given a copy of *Magical Water Plants of the Mediterranean* (author unknown) by Barty Crouch, Jr., disguised as Professor Moody. It is unlikely that this book is commonly referenced in the average Herbology class. Additionally, during their sixth year, Hermione references *Flesh-Eating Trees of the World* (author unknown) to determine the correct way to juice Snargaluff pods.

DID YOU KNOW?

Flourish and Blotts sells a book titled *Encyclopedia of Toadstools*.

DESCRIPTION OF HERBOLOGY CLASSROOM

Herbology is one of three courses that takes place on the Hogwarts grounds rather than in the castle itself. At least two greenhouses are used for the course and are located behind the school. These spaces are built to let light in, meaning the entirety of the classroom is made from glass or a similar material. Each greenhouse contains plants that require various levels of expertise to work with. Plants can be found all over the greenhouses, even hanging from the ceiling in some instances.

The greenhouses have long tables for students to work on to facilitate transplanting seedlings or perform other plant-care tasks as assigned. These tables may be built at a standing level. Different materials are likely stored in the room, as the course requires vastly different supplies than others in the curriculum. Containers of soils, fertilizers and compost are likely spread throughout each greenhouse for easy accessibility. It's probable there are cabinets or shelves to store earmuffs, extra dragon-hide gloves, pruning shears, trowels and any additional supplies either within each greenhouse or directly outside them in a central location. Materials like pots, trays and drip pans might be stacked along the greenhouse walls for convenient storage.

Unlike other courses, Herbology has multiple classrooms, so it's likely each greenhouse features a unique set of tools and equipment depending on the plants studied there. Earmuffs should be stored in the greenhouse with mandrakes, for example, while dragon-hide gloves may be kept with plants that could bite or otherwise puncture the skin. Dangerous plants likely require safety mechanisms like spells or barriers, which could be as simple as additional glass or gates, effectively dividing the greenhouse into two sections. Greenhouses with less dangerous flora may simply have tables filled with plants throughout the space, creating a more immersive classroom environment.

PLANTS AND HERBS DIRECTORY
POTENTIAL RATING SYSTEM
X - Docile & Dull, Harmless
XX - Easily Tamable
XXX - Feasibly Domesticated
XXXX - Dangerous, Specialist Knowledge Required, Could Be Poisonous
XXXXX - Deadly, Should Not Be Approached, Likely Poisonous or Violent in Nature

X

ASPHODEL is a flowering plant used in potions. Its powdered root is used in the Draught of Living Death. Asphodel describes flowers from the genus *Asphodelus*, which have long narrow leaves and flowers that bloom from spikes.

DAISY, also referred to as the English daisy, is a perennial herbaceous plant. Its flowers consist of white petals radiating out from yellow discs, and its roots can be used in the Shrinking Solution.

DITTANY is a powerful healing herb. It can be consumed raw to help heal wounds caused by a variety of situations. When combined with other ingredients, it can be used to mend more significant injuries, like a werewolf bite.

FLUXWEED, or the false pennyroyal, is a type of mustard plant that, when picked on a full moon, is used to make the Polyjuice Potion. Its flower is purple with five petals. It can be toxic when consumed over long periods of time.

GINGER, a brown, irregularly shaped perennial plant with green stems, is used as an ingredient in the Wit-Sharpening Potion and the Beautification Potion. It is also used as an additive to food and beverages.

HORSERADISH, a white irregularly shaped perennial root plant, is an ingredient in Zygmunt Budge's Laughing Potion. They thrive in most conditions.

KNOTGRASS grows readily on the Hogwarts grounds in the Forbidden Forest and is used to make Polyjuice Potion. It has long leaves shaped like ovals and incredibly small white and pink flowers.

LADY'S MANTLE is an herbaceous perennial plant used in Zygmunt Budge's Beautification Potion. Its petalless flowers are green to yellow in color with gray-green leaves.

PEPPERMINT is a perennial hybrid plant that can be used in potion-making. Its leaves are dark green with red veins. During the 1996–1997 school year, Harry adds a sprig of peppermint to his Elixir to Induce Euphoria at the recommendation of Snape's textbook scribblings. This helps counteract some of the potion's side effects, like nose tweaking and excessive singing.

ROSES are a woody perennial plant family used in potion-making. There are several species of roses, though most have five petals on their flowers. They come in a variety of colors, from red to white to yellow. Their petals are used in Zygmunt Budge's Beautification Potion though may also be used in different love potions. Tormentil, a member of the family, is used in Doxycide, a potion used in Doxy removal.

RUE, also called common rue, is a potion ingredient and poison antidote with bluish-green leaves and small yellow flowers. It is used to make Felix Felicis. When Ron suffers the effects of an unintentional love potion during the 1996–1997 school year, Horace Slughorn gives him essence of rue to remedy the effects.

SQUILL is an herbaceous perennial genus of plants that comes in a variety of colors, including blue, pink and white. It is used in potion-making, particularly as a component of Felix Felicis. Squill grows best in partial shade to full sunlight. It flowers in the spring.

THYME, a perennial herb with purple flowers, is used in potion-making. A tincture of the herb is used in Felix Felicis. It flowers from late spring through early summer.

VALERIAN is a perennial flowering plant used in potion-making, particularly to brew the Draught of Living Death. Its sprigs and roots are most commonly used, and its flowers can be white to pink in color.

XX
FLUTTERBY BUSH is a magical plant that quivers. Its leaves can move in a wave-like motion, even without wind. Students work with it during the 1994–1995 school year.

GURDYROOT is a magical plant that resembles an onion but is green in color rather than the traditional yellow, red or white. It can be used to make a drinkable infusion.

LOVAGE is a leafy perennial plant that can cause inflammation of the brain. For this reason, it's used in Confusing and Befuddlement Draughts. Its leaves look like they're divided into three pieces, and its flowers are small, usually yellow or green in color.

MALLOWSWEET is a magical plant used by centaurs in their forms of divination. During the 1995–1996 school year, Firenze directs his Divination students to burn it on the floor of the classroom to look for shapes in the fumes.

MOLY is a powerful, black-stemmed magical plant with white flowers that can be eaten to counteract enchantments.

PLANGENTINE is a magical plant that flowers and/or produces fruit. It is known to have been planted in Godric's Hollow.

SAGE is a perennial shrub with bluish-purple flowers used by centaurs for divination purposes. During the 1995–1996 school year, Firenze has his Divination students burn it on the floor of the classroom to look for shapes in the fumes.

SCREECHSNAP is a magical plant that can move and produce sound. It can be agitated if it is covered in too much fertilizer. Students work with the plants during the 1995–1996 school year.

SCURVY-GRASS is a biennial plant used in Confusing and Befuddlement Draughts due to its ability to cause brain inflammation. It has white flowers with four petals, which can look like a cross, and leaves that can range from dark green to purple in color.

SHRIVELFIG is a magical plant that, when skinned, is used to brew the Shrinking Solution. It is also called the Abyssinian Shrivelfig because Abyssinia, now known as Ethiopia, is where the best plants for brewing are found. Students work with it during the 1992–1993 school year.

SNEEZEWORT is also used in Confusing and Befuddlement Draughts because it can cause brain inflammation. This herbaceous perennial plant has white or yellow flowers that can have anywhere from seven to 15 petals. It can even form double flowers, which can result in three or more layers of more than 20 petals.

SOPOPHOROUS is a magical plant that produces a white bean, which is used in the Draught of Living Death and can release a silver juice when crushed or sliced. It grows best in gloomy marshlands.

XXX
ALIHOTSY is a magical plant that can cause hysteria when consumed in specific amounts. The best way to treat the hysteria is ingesting a Glumbumble syrup. Its leaves are used as an ingredient in Zygmunt Budge's Laughing Potion, though he notes you must not stir the potion too quickly or you risk ruining the

leaves' "mirthful properties." It is also used to flavor fudge.

BELLADONNA, also known as deadly nightshade, is an incredibly poisonous perennial herbaceous plant with green leaves and bell-shaped flowers that can vary from white to purple. It is used in potion-making, and its essence is part of the standard potion-making kit used by Hogwarts students.

BOUNCING BULB is a magical plant known for its active motion. If it is not controlled appropriately, it can hit individuals. Students work with these plants during the 1994–1995 school year.

FANGED GERANIUM is a magical flowering plant with fanged teeth. It can bite individuals attempting to care for it. This plant is a part of the Herbology O.W.L. exam during the 1995–1996 school year.

GILLYWEED is a magical plant found in the Mediterranean Sea that, when consumed, gives an individual gills and webbing between their fingers and toes and allows them to breathe underwater for a period of time.

The grayish-green plant resembles rat tails and has a slimy consistency. Gillyweed is kept in Snape's private store of potion ingredients, meaning it is likely used in potions. Harry eats this plant to breathe underwater as part of the second task of the Triwizard Tournament during the 1994–1995 school year.

HONKING DAFFODIL is a magical plant grown in the Herbology greenhouses by Pomona Sprout. It resembles the mundane daffodil, with six-petaled flowers that can be white, yellow or orange. Unlike mundane daffodils, however, they make a distinct honking sound (which may play on the fact that the mundane daffodil's flowering portion is referred to as a trumpet).

MIMBULUS MIMBLETONIA is an exceedingly rare magical plant native to Assyria that strongly resembles a gray cactus. It is covered in boils instead of spines, which, when prodded, will exude Stinksap. This sap is green in color, and though it smells lik manure, it is not poisonous. It can easily be cleaned up using the Scouring Charm. Stroking the plant once it has matured will cause it to make crooning noises. Neville has one in his care during the 1995–1996 school year, a gift for his 15th birthday, that he hopes to breed.

NIFFLER'S FANCY is a magical plant that gets its name from its shiny copper-tone leaves. It was once used as currency and was thought to be used in potion-making, though its effects aren't well-known. It is a known ingredient of the Potion of All Potential, a potion that can bring out the best in the consumer.

PUFFAPOD is a magical plant that has pink pods filled with shiny beans. If the beans are hit with force, such as when they fall to the floor, they will immediately bloom. Students work with it during the 1993–1994 school year.

WIGGENTREE is a magical rowan that is used in wandmaking by Ollivander. Simply touching the tree can help protect someone against Dark creatures.

XXXX
BUBOTUBER is a magical plant that has the appearance of a black slug. Its swellings are filled with a pus that is yellow-green in color and has a smell similar to gasoline. When diluted, the pus can be used to cure acne or pustules. Undiluted pus can cause boils if it comes in contact with skin.

COWBANE, sometimes called northern water hemlock, is a poisonous perennial herbaceous plant used as an ingredient in Doxycide. It has small white flowers that form in clusters.

HELLEBORE is a poisonous perennial plant used in potion-making, including the Draught of Peace. The term "hellebore" can refer to several varieties of plants housed under the genus *Helleborus*. Its flowers can range from whites to dark, almost black purples.

MANDRAKE is a magical plant used in antidotes. Their roots resemble a human baby. While useful to correct cursed or Transfigured individuals, like those Petrified during Harry's second year, their cry is deadly to any who hear it. Even young plants can render an individual unconscious with their scream.

PRITCHER'S PORRITCH is a rare magical plant that contains pods that exude a lumpy blue substance inside them. The plant is used in the Potion of All Potential.

THAUMATAGORIA is a magical plant that is speculated as mythical by many witches and wizards due to its rarity. It is an ingredient in the Potion of All Potential.

WITCH'S GANGLION is a rare magical plant with a blood-red bulb that may throb. It grows in ponds in the Far East and is used to make the Potion of All Potential.

WORMWOOD is a poisonous herbaceous perennial plant. When combined with asphodel, it creates the Draught of Living Death. Its leaves are grayish-green with a white underside.

XXXXX
ACONITE, also called wolfsbane or monkshood, is a potion ingredient. The genus in which these plants are categorized, *Aconitum*, comprises incredibly poisonous plants, so caution is needed when handling them. Its leaves tend to be dark green. Flowers range from blue to purple and bloom from late summer through early fall.

DEVIL'S SNARE is a magical plant that uses its vines and tendrils to capture individuals. The more someone struggles, the tighter its vines become, which can result in death. Fire can be used to drive it away.

HEMLOCK is an incredibly poisonous herbaceous plant used to make Doxycide. It has small white flowers with five petals each and green leaves with red or purple stems.

SNARGALUFF is a magical tree that has the appearance of a knobbly stump. If disturbed, spike-covered branches sprout out, ready to attack. In the center of the vines are pulsating green pods that excrete worm-like tubers when juiced. Students work with it during the 1996–1997 school year.

VENOMOUS TENTACULA is a magical plant with vines and teeth. A bite from it can cause death. Their seeds are classified as a Class C Non-Tradeable Substance.

PLANTS TAUGHT BY YEAR

FIRST YEAR

First-year Herbology students attend class in greenhouse one, where they primarily learn about the uses and methods of care for various herbs and fungi. Being novices, students are not given hands-on experience with dangerous plants and only learn about them in theory, such as Devil's Snare, which chokes its victims unless driven off by fire.

SECOND YEAR

In their second year, students attend class in greenhouse three, where they are introduced to more dangerous plants that require special protective gear to be handled safely. One of these plants is the mandrake, which is described as a "purplish green," "tufty" humanoid plant that matures from infant into adult over the course of its growth cycle. When pulled out of the ground, it is revealed that the leaves are attached to what looks like a crying baby. Since the mandrake's cry is fatal, soundproof earmuffs must be worn whenever students handle it. Second-year students only interact with seedling mandrakes, whose cry is not yet fatal but can still cause a victim to lose consciousness for several hours. Professor Sprout teaches second-year students how to repot the seedlings. Later in their second year, students learn how to prune Abyssinian Shrivelfigs.

THIRD YEAR

It is safe to assume third-year Herbology introduces students to even more dangerous and exciting plants. Students also learn how to harvest Puffapods.

FOURTH YEAR

In their fourth year, students repot Bouncing Bulbs, which have a tendency to slip from a wizard's hands and smack them in the face. They also prune Flutterby Bushes and learn about the properties of Bubotuber pus (one of which being that it's an excellent acne-buster).

FIFTH YEAR

Students use dragon manure to fertilize plants like Screechsnap seedlings, which squeak and wriggle if too much fertilizer is applied. During the 1995–1996 academic year, fifth-year students have to showcase their herbology knowledge and skills during the O.W.L. exam by handling a Fanged Geranium, which has a tendency to bite.

SIXTH YEAR

Students work with Snargaluff stumps, harvesting pods from them. The Snargaluff comes to life when students try to harvest its pods, attacking them with its thorny vines. They deal with more dangerous plants than in previous years, including the Venomous Tentacula, a dark-red, spiky plant with feelers and teeth that has a horrifying tendency to creep up on students from behind.

SEVENTH YEAR

Students presumably encounter the most dangerous plants during their seventh year of Herbology, after which they take the N.E.W.T. exam to pass the subject, which likely assesses their ability to handle a number of dangerous plants.

MATERIALS REQUIRED FOR HERBOLOGY

Students need various materials and protective equipment to safely interact with the plants covered in Herbology.

- **Bowls** Students use bowls to hold whatever they harvest from plants, like Snargaluff pods.

- **Dragon Dung Compost and Fertilizer** Professor Sprout uses this when she repots plants, preferring it above all other fertilizers.
- **Dragon-Hide Gloves** These are worn to protect students from being injured by dangerous plants.
- **Secateurs** Small, curved-blade pruning tools that can help manage unruly vines. Ron uses secateurs in their sixth year to beat back Snargaluff vines that try to entangle themselves in Hermione's hair.
- **Shears** Used when pruning plants
- **Sound-Proof Earmuffs** A critical necessity when handling mandrakes
- **Trowels** Used to repot plants and sometimes to try to juice Snargaluff pods (Note: It doesn't work very well for the latter.)
- **Wands** For casting charms related to Herbology, like the Severing Charm, to defend against more dangerous plants
- **Watering Cans** Provide optimum plant hydration

MUGGLE COUNTERPARTS FOR MAGICAL PLANTS

DEVIL'S SNARE is one of the scarier plants in the wizarding world, capable of choking its victims. In the Muggle world, there is a plant called *Datura stramonium*, also part of the nightshade family and fairly toxic. It's commonly referred to as jimsonweed. It also doesn't like the sun and only flowers at nighttime. Its seed pods are spiky, giving it a pretty devilish look.

MANDRAKES are known to Muggles as a member of the nightshade family. They are commonly found in the Mediterranean and Middle East and are highly toxic when consumed in large quantities. Many cultures believed these plants had near-magical properties and could cure ailments ranging from gastrointestinal disorders to convulsions and infertility. Some also believed it would help protect those who fought in battle and that it could banish evil spirits or, conversely, be used to create poisons.

WOLFSBANE is a plant used to brew a potion that helps Professor Remus Lupin stay in control of his mind and actions when he turns into a werewolf. Wolfsbane, also referred to as monkshood or aconite, exists in the Muggle world and is deadly to anyone who comes into contact with it. The plant likely got its name thanks to its droopy purple flowers that resemble a monk's hood. Swallowing any part of the plant can be fatal. Wolfsbane was also used to kill wolves in the past, which is likely how the name originated.

WORMWOOD, a key ingredient in the Draught of Living Death, is readily available in the Muggle world. It looks like an herb and is primarily used as a treatment for gastrointestinal ailments and parasites. Surprisingly, Muggles use wormwood in their own "potions," so to speak—liquors like absinthe and vermouth contain wormwood.

History of Magic

From giant wars and goblin rebellions to the Medieval Assembly of European Wizards and the International Warlock Convention of 1289, there are plenty of notable people and events that shaped the course of wizarding history. Just as Hogwarts molds its young minds to comprehend how to perform spells, brew potions and understand the care of various magical entities, the school also prepares students to grasp the sociopolitical forces that influence their world.

HISTORY OF HISTORY OF MAGIC COURSE

It is safe to assume History of Magic has been taught at Hogwarts since the school's inception—there's always history to cover, especially with a Dark wizard like Voldemort on the rise. History of Magic is a compulsory subject for the first five years at Hogwarts and, much like its Muggle counterpart, focuses on significant events that took place in the past that have influenced the present in some way. A specific focus is placed on dates and names.

Professor Cuthbert Binns, Hogwarts's sole ghost professor, leads the class. Due to his incredibly boring teaching style, his monotone lessons make for a mind-numbingly dull experience. During Harry's time at the school, the one notable exception to this rule occurs during the 1992–1993 school year, when Hermione asks Binns about the Chamber of Secrets in response to an attack at the school. He is both surprised and annoyed by her query and at first gives her a curt response: "My subject is History of Magic. I deal with *facts*... not myths and legends." Hermione presses on, though, and Professor Binns eventually shares what he knows about the Chamber of Secrets. It is quite possibly the only time in the history of Professor Binns teaching the class that every student pays attention.

NOTABLE HISTORY OF MAGIC PROFESSORS AND STUDENTS

During Harry's time at Hogwarts, the ghost of **Professor Cuthbert Binns** teaches the course. The length of his tenure is unknown, but it's likely he had been teaching for some time before his death. Hogwarts legend has it that Professor Binns wasn't initially aware he died while dozing off in the Hogwarts staffroom. He simply got up from his chair upon waking, not taking stock of the fact he'd left his body behind.

While there's no doubt Professor Binns is knowledgeable about the subject, he's hardly an ideal professor when it comes to conveying information to his students: Rather than paying attention to his class, he simply reads from his notes during lectures, never asking questions or encouraging participation. The fact that all his students are bored out of their minds doesn't seem to faze him. To add to the teacher/student disconnect, he isn't particularly good at remembering their names, referring to Hermione as "Miss Grant" during the 1992–1993 school year and calling Seamus Finnigan "O'Flaherty." It's likely Professor Binns confuses some of his current students with former students at times.

History of Magic is not a subject at which many students excel, mostly because Professor Binns's droning voice makes it nearly impossible to stay awake. Naturally, this doesn't stop Hermione from getting an O (outstanding) O.W.L. in the subject (but it couldn't have been easy). Given that **Barty Crouch, Jr.,** received 12 O.W.L.s in his fifth year, History of Magic must have been among them. Harry and Ron fail the subject, mostly because they have no interest in it and partly because they never pay attention, often borrowing Hermione's notes for homework assignments and exams. Harry achieves a D (dreadful), which isn't surprising since he sees a troubling vision of Voldemort holding Sirius Black hostage while taking the exam.

REQUIRED HISTORY OF MAGIC TEXTBOOKS BY YEAR

A History of Magic by Bathilda Bagshot is listed on first-year students' list of required textbooks. This text is likely used throughout a student's seven years at Hogwarts given that no extra History of Magic textbooks appear on the school supplies list in subsequent years. Bagshot's book covers the history of the wizarding world from antiquity through the 19th century, including the goblin rebellions, witch hunts, giant wars and Uric the Oddball, among other things.

NOT REQUIRED BUT HELPFUL

Hogwarts: A History by Bathilda Bagshot contains all the known information about Hogwarts within its more than 1,000 pages. Highlights include facts about the school's founders, the Great Hall's enchanted ceiling, how Hogwarts stays hidden from Muggles and why Muggle technology malfunctions in or near the school. One important piece of information the book contains (and that Hermione constantly reminds Harry and Ron of) is that no one can Apparate within or into the Hogwarts grounds. Despite the book's importance, Hermione is likely the only student in her class who has read it from cover to cover, although students take a great interest in it during the 1992–1993 school year when the Chamber of Secrets is reopened. It is available at the Hogwarts library.

The trio consults **Great Wizards of the Twentieth Century** (author unknown) in the Hogwarts library while trying to find information about Nicolas Flamel in their first year.

Great Wizarding Events of the Twentieth Century (author unknown) is a reference book that notes, among other famous names and happenings, that Harry defeated Lord Voldemort as an infant. Hermione consults it before her first year at Hogwarts.

Modern Magical History (author unknown) is a more recent history book Hermione uses to gain insight into the wizarding world that also mentions Harry.

DESCRIPTION OF HISTORY OF MAGIC CLASSROOM

Located on the first floor of Hogwarts Castle, this room is likely quite spacious, given that in 1993, Defense Against the Dark Arts professor Remus Lupin uses it to allow Harry to practice the Patronus Charm on a Boggart.

Since History of Magic solely focuses on theory, the class is laid out with various desks in rows. These are likely placed close together so students can still collaborate and, as Hermione does to Harry and Ron, nudge their peers when they're not paying attention.

The class has a blackboard at the front through which Professor Cuthbert Binns passes when he enters and leaves the room. The class is likely outfitted with various bookshelves containing books related to the subject. The room presumably has several windows with narrow ledges and thick glass. The windows are large enough for owls as big as Hedwig to pass through.

A GENERAL HISTORY OF MAGIC

Magic, like humanity, is believed to have originated in Africa. Ancient Egyptian wizards used curses to protect tombs from plunderers, and Indian wizards created the Snake Summons Spell (aka *Serpensortia*). Dark magic can be traced throughout history, starting with Herpo the Foul, who created the first basilisk and Horcrux in ancient Greece.

The wand was invented in Europe sometime before 382 B.C.E., when Ollivanders was established. Wands have become more commonplace around the world in modernity, but many African wizards cast wandless spells using only hand gestures. When Europeans arrived in North America, they encountered many Native American wizards, who were noted as accomplished Animagi and for their skills in wandless potion-making.

The Department of Mysteries, which predates the Ministry of Magic by at least 35 years, has conducted secret research since 1672 on enigmas such as thought, prophecy, death, love, space and time. Wizardkind has made great leaps in teleportation via Apparition, Portkeys and Floo powder, the third of which was invented in the 13th century. Time travel, accomplished with the aid of a Time-Turner, is trickier and rarely allowed by the government; in one instance, a 19th-century witch named Eloise Mintumble traveled from 1899 to 1402 but was stuck in the past for five days.

The desire to cheat death has motivated many a wizard across the history of magical experimentation, prompting attempts to create Horcruxes and the Sorcerer's Stone. When a witch or wizard dies, they can choose to remain tethered to the living as a ghost, though very few make this choice. The other path is to go "on," and the archway within the Department of Mysteries is theorized to be a portal to an afterlife. Consuming unicorn blood or various potions can also prolong one's life. Harry is the only person who has ever survived the Killing Curse, thanks to the love magic resulting from his mother's sacrifice.

GOBLIN REBELLIONS
Since some witches and wizards hold prejudice that such beings are inferior or uncivilized and should be controlled, goblins have long organized revolts against the wizarding world for placing restrictions on non-human magical beings (e.g., prohibiting wand ownership). Other beings or perceived half-breed humans (e.g., werewolves) have been known to participate in these events. The most prominently studied and violent rebellions occurred in the 17th and 18th centuries. In 1612, one of the Hogsmeade inns served as headquarters for a goblin rebellion. In 1752, Minister of Magic Albert Boot resigned after poorly managing a rebellion. While accounts of these uprisings are sparse in more recent times, tensions between humans and goblins continue in Britain today.

TIME LINE OF KEY EVENTS IN THE MAGICAL WORLD

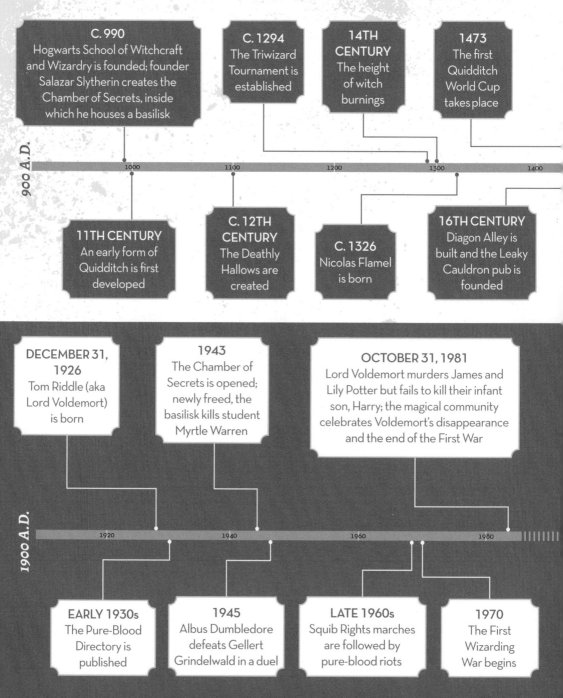

900 A.D.

C. 990
Hogwarts School of Witchcraft and Wizardry is founded; founder Salazar Slytherin creates the Chamber of Secrets, inside which he houses a basilisk

C. 1294
The Triwizard Tournament is established

14TH CENTURY
The height of witch burnings

1473
The first Quidditch World Cup takes place

11TH CENTURY
An early form of Quidditch is first developed

C. 12TH CENTURY
The Deathly Hallows are created

C. 1326
Nicolas Flamel is born

16TH CENTURY
Diagon Alley is built and the Leaky Cauldron pub is founded

1000 1100 1200 1300 1400

1900 A.D.

DECEMBER 31, 1926
Tom Riddle (aka Lord Voldemort) is born

1943
The Chamber of Secrets is opened; newly freed, the basilisk kills student Myrtle Warren

OCTOBER 31, 1981
Lord Voldemort murders James and Lily Potter but fails to kill their infant son, Harry; the magical community celebrates Voldemort's disappearance and the end of the First War

EARLY 1930s
The Pure-Blood Directory is published

1945
Albus Dumbledore defeats Gellert Grindelwald in a duel

LATE 1960s
Squib Rights marches are followed by pure-blood riots

1970
The First Wizarding War begins

1920 1940 1960 1980

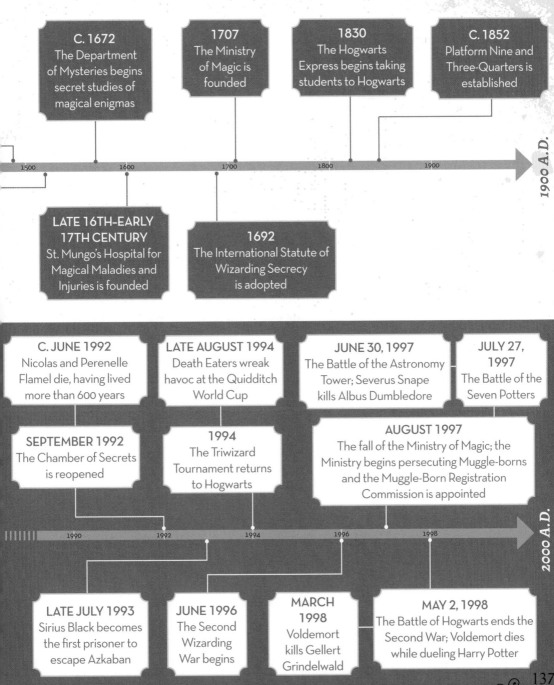

C. 1672
The Department of Mysteries begins secret studies of magical enigmas

1707
The Ministry of Magic is founded

1830
The Hogwarts Express begins taking students to Hogwarts

C. 1852
Platform Nine and Three-Quarters is established

1500 — 1600 — 1700 — 1800 — 1900

1900 A.D.

LATE 16TH–EARLY 17TH CENTURY
St. Mungo's Hospital for Magical Maladies and Injuries is founded

1692
The International Statute of Wizarding Secrecy is adopted

C. JUNE 1992
Nicolas and Perenelle Flamel die, having lived more than 600 years

LATE AUGUST 1994
Death Eaters wreak havoc at the Quidditch World Cup

JUNE 30, 1997
The Battle of the Astronomy Tower; Severus Snape kills Albus Dumbledore

JULY 27, 1997
The Battle of the Seven Potters

SEPTEMBER 1992
The Chamber of Secrets is reopened

1994
The Triwizard Tournament returns to Hogwarts

AUGUST 1997
The fall of the Ministry of Magic; the Ministry begins persecuting Muggle-borns and the Muggle-Born Registration Commission is appointed

1990 — 1992 — 1994 — 1996 — 1998

2000 A.D.

LATE JULY 1993
Sirius Black becomes the first prisoner to escape Azkaban

JUNE 1996
The Second Wizarding War begins

MARCH 1998
Voldemort kills Gellert Grindelwald

MAY 2, 1998
The Battle of Hogwarts ends the Second War; Voldemort dies while dueling Harry Potter

WIZARDS AND WITCHES KNOWN TO THE MUGGLE WORLD

A few of history's most powerful spellcasters were so well-known that even Muggles have heard of them.

CLAUDIUS PTOLEMY

Ptolemy, as he was commonly known, was a first-century wizard Muggle historians recognize as a prolific mathematician, geographer and astronomer. He lived in the ancient city of Alexandria, Egypt. His writings were instrumental even beyond the Greco-Roman world. He was also a wizard, and his Chocolate Frog card is rare.

CIRCE

One can read about an immortal enchantress named Circe in Homer's *The Odyssey*, an important work of ancient Greek mythology for the Muggle community. In the tale, Circe uses magic to transfigure the hero Odysseus's crew into pigs. Historically, she is known as a daughter of Hecate, goddess of witchcraft, and is said to have been a skilled potion-maker and herbologist.

HENGIST OF WOODCROFT

Two brothers whom Muggles celebrate in British mythology are Hengist and Horsa. They are said to have led a wave of Germanic invaders who settled near Kent in the fifth century. What Muggles don't know is that Hengist was a wizard. While attending Hogwarts, Hengist was Sorted into Hufflepuff House; he later went down in wizarding history as the founder of the village of Hogsmeade.

MERLIN

The name Merlin comes to mind for most Muggles when they are asked to think of a wizard. Traditionally, when imagining Merlin one envisions an old man with long white hair and beard wearing a cloak (not unlike Albus Dumbledore). A well-known figure in British folklore, Merlin appears in medieval tales as a member of King Arthur's court. Though

Muggles consider him fictitious, in actuality, Merlin was a prominent and powerful member of the wizarding community. He notably attended Hogwarts as a Slytherin. It is for him that the Order of Merlin was named, and the green color of the ribbon designating a First Class recipient is believed to represent his Hogwarts House. Today, his name is often heard as part of common exclamations such as "Merlin's Beard!"

NICOLAS FLAMEL
Muggles believe Flamel was a 14th-century French bookseller who attempted to practice alchemy (for more information, see pg. 43).

PARACELSUS
Philippus Aureolus Theophrastus Bombastus von Hohenheim, aka Paracelsus, was a famous physician and philosopher known to Muggle historians familiar with the German Renaissance. His contributions to medicine are well-documented, and he is often called the Father of Toxicology. He was also a celebrated wizard and alchemist; at Hogwarts, a bust of Paracelsus sits in a corridor en route to the owlery. Like others on this list, he also has his own Chocolate Frog card.

Muggle Studies

Though they operate mostly in wizarding society, students at Hogwarts benefit from learning about the history and daily lives of their non-magical neighbors, namely how they can survive without magic. The class covers Muggle technologies, science and significant historical events of the non-magical world.

HISTORY OF MUGGLE STUDIES COURSE

It is unknown when Hogwarts first offered Muggle Studies. Since Professor Quirinus Quirrell taught the subject before leaving on sabbatical in 1990, the class has most likely been part of the curriculum from at least the 1980s onward.

Muggle Studies is an elective taught from third to seventh year. There is both an O.W.L. and a N.E.W.T. examination for the subject. Though some wizards consider Muggle Studies to be a soft option, Percy Weasley disagrees. He points out that understanding Muggles can be important when seeking a job that deals with the non-magical community. In fact, since most of the work the Ministry of Magic does involves hiding wizarding existence from Muggles, it is reasonable to assume most careers in the government require at least a basic understanding of the non-magical community.

Muggle relations in itself is a career path Hogwarts students may choose after graduation. A pamphlet handed to fifth-year students in 1996 during their career advice meetings states a passing O.W.L. grade is required to pursue a career in Muggle relations.

During the 1997–1998 school year, Death Eater Alecto Carrow takes over the class and uses it as a propaganda tool for Voldemort's regime with the intention of brainwashing young witches and wizards into hating Muggles and Muggle-borns.

After the second wizarding war, it is assumed the subject returns to its original purpose: promoting awareness and understanding between the magical and non-magical communities.

NOTABLE MUGGLE STUDIES PROFESSORS AND STUDENTS

Due to Voldemort's rise to and fall from power in the 1990s, Hogwarts has cycled through more Muggle Studies professors than for any other subject save Defense Against the Dark Arts (see pg. 93)

In the 1980s, **Quirinus Quirrell** taught the class before leaving to go on sabbatical in 1990. Upon his return, he begins teaching Defense Against the Dark Arts—but he's hardly the same. During his travels, Quirrell had come across a forest in Albania where a much-weakened Voldemort was in hiding. Voldemort attached himself to Quirrell, sharing the young teacher's body like a parasite.

During Harry's time at the school in the 1990s, **Charity Burbage**

QUIRRELL: FROM MUGGLE STUDIES TEACHER TO MUGGLE-HATING VOLDEMORT FOLLOWER?

Professor Quirrell did not come across Voldemort's Albania hiding spot by pure chance. His sabbatical was a cover for a very intentional quest to find Voldemort.

Having been timid and nervous while at school, Quirrell found himself feeling insignificant and had a longing to prove himself to others. He thought that if he found the missing Voldemort, it would give him an air of importance, believing that maybe he could learn something from the powerful wizard that would ensure he was taken seriously. However, Quirrell was naive to think he could control Voldemort, even in such a weakened state.

When Quirrell came to the forest where Voldemort was hiding, Voldemort attached himself to the young teacher. Under Voldemort's control, Quirrell attempts to get his hands on the Sorcerer's Stone to return Voldemort to his own body and full power. Harry thwarts Quirrell by acquiring the Stone, and the professor dies after struggling with Harry.

teaches the subject. It is unclear if she took over the job immediately after Quirrell went on sabbatical or if there had been another teacher at the post during that time.

In 1997, Burbage writes an op-ed for the *Daily Prophet* in which she defends Muggles and Muggle-borns, which angers Voldemort. Later, she is captured by Death Eaters and brought to Malfoy Manor. During a meeting between Voldemort and his inner circle, Voldemort murders Burbage by casting the Killing Curse, offering her corpse to Nagini.

When the *Daily Prophet* announces Burbage has "resigned" her post, **Alecto Carrow** is appointed to the position. In a Death Eater-controlled Hogwarts, Muggle Studies becomes compulsory. Rather than fostering understanding, the curriculum encourages students to hate and fear Muggles.

Carrow uses the class to brainwash wizarding students into joining Voldemort's cause. She instructs students that Muggles are nothing more than animals and that they had forced wizards into hiding by being vicious toward them.

Before the subject becomes compulsory, known students include Hermione Granger, Bill Weasley, Percy Weasley and Ernie Macmillan. It is likely that Arthur Weasley took Muggle Studies as an elective, given his love for all things Muggle.

REQUIRED MUGGLE STUDIES TEXTBOOKS BY YEAR

Home Life and Social Habits of British Muggles by Wilhelm Wigworthy is an "enormous" book assigned by Professor Burbage. It seems to be relied on rather heavily for homework: During the 1993–1994 school year, third years are assigned hundreds of pages of reading from the text. During a boisterous after-Quidditch party in Gryffindor Tower celebrating Gryffindor's win over Ravenclaw in 1994, a stressed Hermione consults the book in an attempt to finish 422 pages of assigned reading.

DESCRIPTION OF MUGGLE STUDIES CLASSROOM

The Muggle Studies classroom is likely located on the first floor of Hogwarts because, while ascending the marble staircase in 1994, Hermione parts ways with Harry and Ron at the first floor to go to Muggle Studies. Taking into account the considerable amount of textbook work known to exist for the course, there is likely a large theoretical component to Muggle Studies. The classroom is likely configured in the traditional manner, with rows of desks facing a blackboard.

When learning about Muggle technology and devices, those items are likely included in the classroom. Collections of Muggle artifacts may be housed on bookshelves around the classroom walls, perhaps pulled out for some hands-on learning. Even if Muggle technology doesn't operate properly in Hogwarts, it could be useful for students to be able to hold and identify such objects—telephones, spark plugs, garden hoses and so on. A bin on the teacher's desk may contain ballpoint pens for students to use during class instead of the standard-issue quills favored by witches and wizards.

TIME LINE OF MUGGLE EVENTS
THAT AFFECTED THE WIZARDING WORLD

As a result of living side by side, at times more peacefully than others, wizards and Muggles naturally have some overlapping chapters in their history books.

Throughout antiquity and the Middle Ages, witches and wizards were more open about displaying their powers in the presence of the non-magical community. Whether thrilled or terrified by magic, Muggles understood that various tools—cauldrons, wands, broomsticks and others—are associated with magic. Likewise, most Muggles possessed an awareness of magical beasts such as dragons and unicorns and beings such as giants and mermaids.

During the 14th to 18th centuries, however, Muggles in Europe and North America began fearing the abilities of their wizarding neighbors, hunting them down and persecuting them. The effectiveness of witch hunts is questionable, considering many Muggles were sentenced to death for magical abilities they did not possess, and on the off-chance a true witch or wizard was apprehended, they were typically able to escape being burned at the stake by casting Flame-Freezing Charms. According to historian Bathilda Bagshot, this charm would make the flames harmless. The witch or wizard being "burned" would pretend to shriek with pain while enjoying a tickling sensation. Wendelin the Weird enjoyed it so much that she allowed herself to be caught 47 times in different disguises.

The Salem witch trials that occurred in Massachusetts in 1692 and 1693 were particularly devastating to the magical community. Though most judges in these trials were Puritan leaders, according to wizarding history, some were actually wizards, known as Scourers, who used the Muggles' hysteria to hunt down specific individuals as a means of settling personal vendettas. As a result, many wizarding families left America and wizarding immigration to the States slowed.

In Europe, wizards formed exclusive communities like Godric's Hollow in an attempt to stay safe among their own. The increasing severity of witch hunts contributed to the signing of the International Statute of Secrecy in 1689 and led to the creation of the British Ministry of Magic.

OTHER SIGNIFICANT CROSSOVER EVENTS BETWEEN THESE COMMUNITIES INCLUDE...

- A wizard named Armand Malfoy participated in the Norman Conquest in the 11th century. Malfoy provided devious magical services to William the Conqueror in exchange for land. Elizabeth I is believed to have turned down the marital aspirations of the first Lucius Malfoy, who may have jinxed the queen, resulting in her decision to never marry.
- In 1620, the Mayflower's voyage from England to the New World brought more than pilgrims to Massachusetts. The founder of Ilvermorny School of Witchcraft and Wizardry, Isolt Sayre, stowed away on the ship to escape her evil aunt, Gormlaith Gaunt. Isolt left the Plymouth settlement among the Puritans and moved to Mount

Greylock, where she would later build Ilvermorny.

- In 1804, Richard Trevithick launched the first steam-powered train, changing travel for Muggles and wizards alike. With broomstick sightings risking the International Statute of Secrecy, the limitations of the Floo Network and the logistical problems of traveling with underage wizards, trains became an alternative means of transport for the magical community. The Hogwarts Express transports underage students to and from Hogwarts, and the Great Wizarding Express is known to have run between England and Berlin in the 1930s.

- During the American Revolution, Minister of Magic Porteus Knatchbull was asked by his Muggle counterpart, Lord North, to do something about King George III's declining mental health. Subsequent allegations that Lord North believed in wizards contributed to his resignation in 1782.

- Minister of Magic Evangeline Orpington was friendly with Queen Victoria. Orpington's interference is believed to have influenced the Crimean War of the 1850s, a conflict that had far-reaching implications, setting the stage for World War I.

- In 1858, Priscilla Dupont was obliged to step down as Minister of Magic as a result of her excessive pranking of Prime Minister Lord Palmerston, whom the Muggles also forced to resign.

- Minister of Magic Archer Evermonde passed legislation forbidding wizards from getting involved in World War I, but some wizards defied this order. Magizoologist Newt Scamander joined a force of wizards who worked with the dragon population on the Eastern Front, while his brother, Theseus Scamander, earned the designation of "war hero" for his involvement.

- The Second World War and the Global Wizarding War occurred simultaneously: While the Allies fought Nazi Germany, Dark wizard Gellert Grindelwald proselytized similar hateful ideologies among the wizarding community. Ultimately, both conflicts ended in 1945 when Germany and Japan surrendered and Albus Dumbledore defeated

Grindelwald in a duel. A good working relationship was maintained between Prime Minister Winston Churchill and Minister of Magic Leonard Spencer-Moon, who held their respective posts throughout the conflict.

How Muggles Live Without Magic

Harry learns much about the way Muggles conduct their daily business while growing up with the Dursleys and during his summer breaks away from Hogwarts. He watches them cook with pots and pans (even jumping in at Petunia's order to whip up a batch of bacon), watch television and drive cars. Harry and the Dursleys also take a rowboat to reach the hut on the rock in 1991. Rather than rely on owl post, Petunia uses a phone to communicate with people. She also dyes clothing in a sink rather than casting a spell to change its color. Washing the car, mowing the lawn and painting a bench all require different sets of materials that aren't just a wave of a wand, all of which include quite a bit of physical labor. These tasks take time and a bit of prior planning to carry out.

When the Weasley family, Harry and Hermione attend the Quidditch World Cup in 1994, they camp like Muggles. Once they magically extend their tents, Arthur won't let them use magic to cook or get water, preferring they cook over a campfire and fetch water from a pump, as Muggles do.

The Use of Muggle Objects Within the Wizarding World

While they won't always admit it, wizards have co-opted some Muggle technology for their benefit.

One of the most significant Muggle artifacts used in the wizarding world is the train. The Hogwarts Express, still driven by a conductor, shuttles students to and from Hogwarts and first began service after the enactment of the International Statute of Secrecy. Before the Statute was put in place, students employed all manner of ways of reaching the school, including broomstick, enchanted carriage and

Apparition. The use of Portkeys, which continued for a time after the Statute was passed, proved to be a logistical nightmare that would fill the hospital wing with sick students, prompting the Ministry to find a safer, less chaotic means of transport. A stack of paperwork, a humongous Concealment Charm and 167 Memory Charms later, the government acquired a Muggle steam engine they then modified according to their needs (although for whatever reason, they neglected to make it a fully automated, self-driving train).

Radios, the Muggle device for listening to news and music, are also used by wizards. The Weasleys keep a radio in their home next to the kitchen sink that plays Celestina Warbeck tunes during Christmas. Radios are also used to spread information during the war when many wizards who oppose Voldemort go on the run. *Potterwatch*, a radio program hosted by Lee Jordan, is their primary means of staying up to date on the latest information. A password is required to tune in, meaning only those who know the right people can benefit from its intel.

Wizards use many other objects of Muggle origin, including kettles, knitting needles and tents. It's common to use magic to enhance an object, like charming a kettle to boil instantly with the tap of a wand (as Lupin does in 1993) or tents that offer considerably more square footage than their appearance would suggest, like the ones Harry and the Weasleys use while camping during the 1994 Quidditch World Cup.

MUGGLE OBJECTS INFLUENCED BY THE WIZARDING WORLD

In addition to the Hogwarts Express, Arthur Weasley's flying Ford Anglia is one of the most notable Muggle objects influenced by magic. While Arthur originally told Molly he bought the car to take it apart to better understand how it works, he was in fact charming it to fly and giving it an Invisibility Booster. In 1992, Fred, George and Ron borrow the car to rescue Harry from his home on Privet Drive. Ron and Harry use it again after Dobby blocks them from reaching the train platform. After the friends crash the Ford Anglia into the Whomping Willow, the car drives itself into the Forbidden Forest to continue a life of its own.

It makes one last return later that school year to save Harry, Ron and Fang from being devoured by Aragog's hungry brood.

This is far from the only charmed Muggle object that Arthur deals with, however—he also comes across a biting tea kettle, shrinking keys, a hiccuping toaster, several regurgitating toilets and a tea set that attacks its new owners after being accidentally sold to a Muggle following its previous owner's death.

ARTHUR WEASLEY: THE MUGGLE WORLD'S BIGGEST FAN

Arthur Weasley is probably the wizarding world's most ardent Muggle enthusiast. When Harry first meets Arthur in 1992, the Weasley patriarch is employed in the Misuse of Muggle Artifacts office at the Ministry of Magic. During his time with the office, he helps author the Muggle Protection Act, likely designed to protect Muggles from objects charmed or otherwise modified by wizards.

Muggle welfare aside, authoring this act gives Arthur the opportunity to include a loophole that allows him to continue his tinkering with Muggle objects so long as the modified items' magical properties aren't intended to be used. It's the perfect career path for him, but not even Arthur could have planned for his sons to take his charmed flying car across the country on a mission to rescue their friend. So strong is his passion for all things made by non-magical people, however, that when an enraged Molly wants him to show his disapproval of their sons' dangerous act, his first instinct is to ask how well his tinkering worked (much to her disappointment).

Knowing Harry was raised in a Muggle household, Arthur never shies away from asking the Boy Who Lived about Muggles. When given the opportunity, however, Arthur will just as readily go straight to the source: Upon meeting Hermione's parents in 1992, he looks on as the Grangers exchange their Muggle pounds for wizard currency, calling Molly over to to see the 10-pound notes. He insists they must get a drink, presumably so he can pick their brains on everything Muggle, much as he does whenever he sees Harry.

Arthur's greatest Muggle interest appears to be electricity. His collection of batteries, his need to confirm the use of plugs in different Muggle objects and his general interest in anything that runs on electricity seems to affirm this. When Harry visits Arthur's office in 1995, he notices posters of cars, a diagram showing how someone should wire a plug and illustrations of post office boxes. Though Arthur is never quite sure how to pronounce "electricity," he certainly enjoys learning about it.

In 1996, the Weasley patriarch is named Head of the Office for the Detection and Confiscation of Counterfeit Defensive Spells and Protective Objects, overseeing 10 wizards tasked with seizing items that falsely claim to protect against Dark magic. It's a decent title bump and important work for the Ministry during wartime, but Molly notes he misses his work with Muggle objects.

Potions

Spells aren't the sole means of performing magic, and enchanted brews can sometimes achieve what charms alone cannot. Young wizards must learn to harness the power of combining magical and mundane ingredients and utilizing the phases of the moon to create draughts that heal, harm or otherwise "ensnare the senses," according to Hogwarts's resident Potions Master, Severus Snape.

HISTORY OF POTIONS COURSE

Potions is one of the seven mandatory courses Hogwarts students take during their first five years, although they can choose to continue the subject in their sixth and seventh years if they achieve the necessary grade on their O.W.L. exams.

The course covers a variety of different potions and potion-related subjects, such as antidotes, ingredient preparation and properties, and other topics that potion brewers may find useful and important. It's likely students learn the significance of brewing times and heat.

During the first couple of years, students learn how to brew various potions while also studying different potion ingredients and their properties. Homework assignments can include writing essays on a variety of topics, such as ingredients and brewing.

At the end of their fifth year, all Hogwarts students take the Potions O.W.L., which consists of a written and a practical portion. For the written portion, students answer questions about potions and their purposes. It's likely there are questions about ingredients and their properties as well. The practical portion likely requires students to prepare the necessary ingredients and brew a potion, with a proctor observing technique.

As students continue to N.E.W.T. level, they begin to brew more complex potions like the Draught of Living Death and learn to develop antidotes to poisons using Golpalott's Third Law. Essays continue to cement students' knowledge of various potions and topics.

Students interested in pursuing a career as a Healer or Auror need an "Exceeds Expectations" or "Outstanding" on their O.W.L.s and N.E.W.T.s.

NOTABLE POTIONS PROFESSORS AND STUDENTS

Professor Severus Snape teaches Potions at Hogwarts for most of his adult life and displays a special talent for the subject. As a student at Hogwarts, he made notes in his personal copy of *Advanced Potion-Making* that improved the existing brewing instructions. A Death Eater who renounced his ways when his allegiance with Voldemort cost him the love of his life, Lily Potter, Snape offered his services to Dumbledore, who put him to work spying on Voldemort while teaching Potions at Hogwarts. He is well accomplished in his career, often called upon by the headmaster and other staff members to brew complicated concoctions such as the Wolfsbane Potion.

During the 1996–1997 academic year, Snape's predecessor, **Professor Horace Slughorn**, comes out of retirement to return to his post while Snape teaches Defense Against the Dark Arts. Like Snape, Slughorn is a skilled potion-maker, brewing complex potions such as Amortentia and Felix Felicis for students to study and observe.

Slughorn held Harry's mother, Lily, in high regard when she was a student at Hogwarts due to her skill. When Harry successfully brews the best Draught of Living Death among his peers, Slughorn exclaims he must have inherited Lily's talent, as she was a "dab hand" at the subject.

Hermione is particularly skilled in Potions. During her second year, she successfully brews a Polyjuice Potion (granted, she makes an error regarding the essence of the person she's trying to transform into, but the potion itself works), which requires quite a bit of skill and patience. She consistently receives positive remarks on her brewing abilities, earning an "Outstanding" on the O.W.L.

Other students who continue on to N.E.W.T.-level Potions with the trio during the 1996–1997 school year include Draco Malfoy, Theodore Nott, Blaise Zabini, Michael Corner, Terry Boot and Ernie Macmillan, meaning they have earned at least an "Exceeds Expectations" on the O.W.L. exam.

REQUIRED POTIONS TEXTBOOKS BY YEAR

Magical Drafts and Potions by Arsenius Jigger is the first Potions textbook used by Hogwarts students. It is on the required list of materials for first years and is likely used through the first five years of school. Jigger is known for his work in not only Potions but also Transfiguration.

Advanced Potion-Making by Libatius Borage is used by N.E.W.T.-level students. It contains information and brewing instructions for several potions, including the Draught of Living Death, the Elixir to Induce Euphoria, Everlasting Elixirs and the Hiccuping Solution. The textbook also has a chapter on antidotes and discusses Golpalott's Third Law, which describes what an antidote to a poison should consist of. Borage notably attended Castelobruxo, the Brazilian wizarding school. He is the author of several different potions books, including *Asiatic Anti-Venoms* and *Have Yourself a Fiesta in a Bottle!* These books are not required reading at Hogwarts, and it is unknown if they are available in the library. His potion recipes, while satisfactory based on Slughorn's feedback to students, have their flaws. In Harry's borrowed copy of *Advanced Potion-Making*, notes made by a young Severus Snape noticeably improve the author's recipes.

DESCRIPTION OF POTIONS CLASSROOM

Beginning in their first year, students must descend to the dungeons for Potions classes.

Unlike other, above-ground classrooms, the Potions environment is dark and dank. Vapors from the bubbling or hissing cauldrons can fog up the air in the room, frequently accompanied by pleasant or foul scents, all of which can prove overwhelming. Adding to the discomfort, the dungeons are quite cold, so much so that students' breath turns to vapor in frigid winter as they huddle around their cauldrons' fires to keep warm. Given that it's an underground room, there are no windows. The walls are lined with jars in which slimy, pickled creatures float.

The classroom is large enough to fit two Houses of students in the same year as well as all of their equipment (cauldrons, scales, phials, etc.). The dungeon room is also outfitted with a blackboard and a teacher's desk. There is a supply cupboard for storing ingredients and spare textbooks, including Snape's own copy of *Advanced Potion-Making*. Students work in pairs or groups, seated upon stools at various tables to prepare ingredients, brew and study their handiwork. Prior to their first year, each student is required to purchase a set of brass scales and a pewter cauldron, standard size 2 (for more on required Potions materials, see pg. 154). Students do not need to haul their equipment to class; it seems the cauldrons remain in the classroom, possibly magically stored away when not in use.

PREPARING POTIONS INGREDIENTS

Students must be meticulous about the ingredients they add to their cauldrons. Not only does each potion have a specific recipe that must be followed, but there is also much to gain by studying the properties of each ingredient. Albus Dumbledore, for instance, discovered the 12 uses of dragon's blood, and among these are multiple occasions for cleaning and healing. Students must also follow instructions carefully as the amount, method and timing of steps must be precise in order to achieve the desired results. In some cases, a small mistake such as adding ingredients in the wrong order or in the wrong quantity can not just ruin a potion but create a poisonous or corrosive mixture. For example, bubotuber pus, a cure for acne, can actually cause the affliction to significantly worsen if not diluted.

Some of Harry's friends learn this lesson the hard way: In a class during the 1993–1994 school year, Neville Longbottom botches his Shrinking Solution by adding too much rat spleen and leech juice, turning what would've been an acid-green brew into an orange one. The results would have been dangerous if he'd fed it to his toad, Trevor, but Hermione's quick advice helps him correct the mistake. Another example of an unwanted result is seen when porcupine quills are added to a Cure for Boils while the cauldron is still over a burning fire. Neville and Seamus Finnigan make this error in 1991; Seamus's cauldron melts and the bubbling potion spills onto the floor, burning students' shoes.

Since potion-making is a particularly temperamental art, it doesn't help that some textbooks contain less than optimal instructions. Snape's old copy of *Advanced Potion-Making* is heavily annotated with alternative advice, documenting his own discoveries for methods that yield more effective results. This may be why he often chooses to provide his own recipes on the blackboard rather than direct his students to their textbooks. In Harry's sixth year, he reads the Half-Blood Prince's inscription that crushing sopophorous beans is a better way of releasing the juices needed for the Draught of Living Death than cutting them, which the textbook advises.

MATERIALS REQUIRED FOR POTIONS

When young witches and wizards turn 11, they receive their Hogwarts letter, which includes a list of equipment for their time at the school.
The equipment necessary for potion-making includes the following:
- 1 set of brass scales
- 1 cauldron (pewter, standard size 2)
- 1 set of glass or crystal phials
- 1 wand

Additional class materials include knives, a mortar and pestle, parchment, quills and ingredients.

When Harry goes on his very first shopping trip in Diagon Alley, he is tempted to spend his newfound wealth on a solid gold cauldron. Hagrid pushes back against this desire, pointing out that the school list specifies pewter. A cauldron made of gold might yield different results for potion-making, but it's also possible Hagrid is trying to spare Harry of the staring and potential ridicule he might face by showing up to school with a wildly expensive school supply. One can also buy other gimmicky cauldrons such as self-stirring or collapsible. All cauldrons are enchanted to be lighter to carry. Cauldron thickness is a point of debate within the Ministry of Magic, as too thin a cauldron may be burned through, with disastrous consequences.

Glass or crystal phials are used to contain small amounts of potions and can store liquids over long periods of time. Brass scales are necessary for weighing exact measurements of ingredients. These ingredients—ranging from herbs to animal parts—might also be crushed, sliced or diced with a mortar and pestle or a knife.

Many ingredients are available in the classroom's storage cupboard, but students typically maintain their own storage of ingredients, which can be purchased at the Apothecary in Diagon Alley. Ingredients may include plants such as ginger root and scurvy grass, animal parts such as spine of lionfish and dragon's blood and inorganic materials such as mooonstone. These ingredients might be infused, powdered or otherwise prepared before use. Some ingredients are more common while others are rare, and a prudent Potions Master will take notice if they go missing. Some can be taken from a plant or animal without harming it while others can only be extracted after death.

POTIONS DIRECTORY

AGING POTION
Effects Causes the drinker to grow older. The strength depends on the amount consumed; the more one drinks, the older they become. A single drop will age a person by a few months
Limitations The effects can be reversed, and they are likely temporary. The effects will not fool an Age Line.

AMORTENTIA
Effects Causes a powerful feeling of infatuation or romantic obsession, overriding one's senses; it smells like whatever scents each individual finds most appealing.
Antidote A clear liquid containing unknown substances
Limitations Banned at Hogwarts

BABBLING BEVERAGE
Effects Causes the drinker to spout nonsense

BEAUTIFICATION POTION
Effects Causes the drinker to become more lovely or visually appealing
Ingredients Fairy wings, morning dew, rose petals, lady's mantle, unicorn tail hair, ginger roots

BLOOD-REPLENISHING POTION
Effects Works like a blood transfusion, restoring the drinker's health after great blood loss

BOIL CURE
Effects Resolves the drinker's boil condition
Ingredients Dried nettles, crushed snake fangs, stewed horned slugs, porcupine quills
Notes on Preparation Porcupine quills must be added after taking the cauldron off the fire.
Year Taught First year

CALMING DRAUGHT
Effects Calms the drinker's nerves or distress

CONFUSING AND BEFUDDLEMENT DRAUGHTS
Effects Causes brain inflammation and produces hot-headedness in the drinker
Ingredients Sneezewort, scurvy grass, lovage

COUGH POTION
Effects Causes the drinker's cough to subside

DEATH POTION
Effects Causes a victim to revisit positive memories, calming and distracting them; once the potion is touched, it thickens and rises to engulf and destroy the victim.
Ingredients Memories
Notes on Preparation Memories may be added last.
Limitations The thickening and rising is slow-moving.

DOXYCIDE
Effects Causes paralysis when sprayed on Doxies

Ingredients Bundimun, dragon liver, Streelers, cowbane essence, hemlock essence, tormentil tincture
Limitations One should cover their nose and mouth when administering.

DRAUGHT OF LIVING DEATH

Effects Causes the drinker to fall into a very deep sleep
Ingredients Asphodel in an infusion of wormwood, valerian roots, sopophorous bean
Notes on Preparation According to *Advanced Potion-Making*, sopophorous beans are supposed to be cut, but crushing them with the side of the knife's blade is more effective at releasing the juices; additionally, a clockwise stir should be added after every seventh counterclockwise stir.
Year Taught Sixth year
Limitations The official instructions are not the most effective.

DRAUGHT OF PEACE

Effects Causes a calming sensation in anxious or agitated individuals
Ingredients Powdered moonstone, syrup of hellebore
Year Taught Fifth year

ELIXIR OF LIFE

Effects Extends one's life for as long as one continues to drink it
Ingredients The Sorcerer's Stone
Notes on Preparation Involves a complicated alchemical process
Limitations Must be continually and regularly drunk or else the person will eventually die of old age; does not maintain the drinker's physique

ELIXIR TO INDUCE EUPHORIA

Effects Causes the drinker to become excitable and happy; side effects include excessive singing and nose-tweaking.
Notes on Preparation Adding peppermint may counterbalance side effects.
Year Taught Sixth year

EVERLASTING ELIXIR
Effects May never run out or always remain potent
Year Taught Sixth year

FELIX FELICIS
Effects Causes the drinker to succeed in their endeavors until the effects wear off; side effects may include "giddiness, recklessness, and dangerous overconfidence" if consumed in excess.
Notes on Preparation A miniscule phial can remain effective for 12 hours.
Year Taught Sixth year
Limitations Must not be consumed in large quantities; banned during exams and organized competitions

FIRE PROTECTION POTION
Effects Allows the drinker to walk through fire unharmed

FLESH-EATING SLUG REPELLENT
Effects Treats a flesh-eating slug infestation

FORGETFULNESS POTION
Effects May either cause or treat forgetfulness
Year Taught First year

HAIR-RAISING POTION
Effects Causes the drinker's hair to stand on end
Ingredients Rat tails
Year Taught Second year

HICCUPING SOLUTION
Effects Likely causes hiccups

MANDRAKE RESTORATIVE DRAUGHT
Effects Revives victims who have been Petrified by a basilisk

Ingredients Mandrake
Notes on Preparation Mandrakes must be mature

PEPPERUP POTION
Effects A remedy for the common cold; warms a chilled person;
a side effect is steam emitting from the drinker's ears.

SHRINKING SOLUTION
Effects Causes things to shrink in size; can also reverse aging
Ingredients Daisy roots, Abyssinian Shrivelfigs, caterpillars, rat spleen, leech juice, infusion of wormwood, cowbane essence
Notes on Preparation Daisy roots must be chopped evenly; adding too much rat spleen or leech juice will turn the potion orange instead of bright acid green.
Year Taught Third year

SKELE-GRO
Effects Causes a drinker's bones to regrow; takes about eight hours to complete the painful process; burns the mouth

SLEEKEAZY'S HAIR POTION
Effects Causes the drinker's hair to become more manageable
(e.g., easing friz)

SLEEPING DRAUGHT
Effects Causes the drinker to sleep
Ingredients Wormwood, valerian, Flobberworm mucus, sopophorous bean, powdered asphodel petals, essence of nettle

STRENGTHENING SOLUTION
Effects Increases a drinker's physical or magical strength
Ingredients Salamander blood, pomegranate juice

Notes on Preparation If brewed poorly, the potion will congeal
and smell of burned rubber.
Year Taught Fifth year

SWELLING SOLUTION

Effects Causes something to grow in size **Ingredients** Pufferfish eyes
Notes on Preparation Explodes when a firecracker is added to it
Year Taught Second year
Antidote Deflating Draught

VERITASERUM

Effects Forces the drinker to tell the truth, such as revealing secrets;
just three drops are needed.
Notes on Preparation Takes a full moon cycle to mature
Limitations Colorless and odorless, not easily detectable when added to
a beverage; controlled by strict Ministry of Magic guidelines; effects can be
blocked using strong Occlumency.

VOLDEMORT'S CAVE POTION

Effects Causes a burning sensation; causes the drinker mental distress,
presumably reliving their worst memories; causes the drinker to wish to stop
drinking the potion; eventually results in a strong thirst for water

WIT-SHARPENING POTION

Effects Causes the drinker to think more clearly and focus more easily
Ingredients Armadillo bile, scarab beetles, ginger roots
Year Taught Fourth year

WOLFSBANE POTION

Effects Eases the effects of lycanthropy so that werewolves may
retain their clear human mind during transformation on the night
of a full moon; tastes awful

Limitations Does not cure the condition of lycanthropy; only effective when consumed before the monthly transition begins

WOUND-CLEANING POTION
Effects Cleans a person's open wounds; stings when applied

HOW EQUIPMENT AFFECTS BREWING

Certain equipment can yield different results for potion-making. While the Hogwarts supplies list specifies brass scales, silver scales may be more effective for weighing ingredients. Brass scales are sold in Diagon Alley.

The Hogwarts list provides students the option of purchasing glass or crystal phials for potion storage. It's unknown whether one type of phial preserves potions more effectively or if the difference between the two materials boils down to aesthetic preference.

The school supply list for first-year students specifically lists cauldrons made from pewter. However, one can purchase other materials in Diagon Alley such as iron, copper, brass, silver, and solid gold. Each type of cauldron would likely be priced according to its speed and efficiency in brewing potions. Gold is not advised, as it may be particularly showy and expensive.

Wizards have dabbled with unusual materials for cauldron crafting, such as Humphrey Belcher, who unsuccessfully attempted to make a cheese cauldron.

THE ETHICS OF LOVE POTIONS

It's no secret that love potions, which are designed to make anyone who consumes them feel besotted or obsessed with the person who administered them, are banned at Hogwarts. This is certainly for the best at a school filled with magically inclined teenagers who are just as susceptible to hormones as their Muggle counterparts. Despite this rule, minors can buy these potions at Weasleys' Wizard Wheezes, and students at Hogwarts have access to the necessary ingredients to brew them in secret. Outside of school, however, adult witches and wizards are free to use love potions as they wish. There are no strict laws regulating their use, which begs the question: Why is a potion that unknowingly afflicts its unconsenting drinker with an infatuation for any one person not regulated by the law?

The creation and use of love potions appears to be a considerable moral and ethical gray area in the magical community—at least to us Muggles. In 1996, Fred and George inform Ginny their potion lasts up to 24 hours; it's unknown whether or not this is the case with all love potions, but no one bats an eye at this sizable time frame. That same year, when Professor Slughorn introduces his N.E.W.T. students to Amortentia—one of the strongest love potions known to wizardkind—he cautions that it's not only powerful but also dangerous. This begs the question: Why are students encouraged to learn how to brew these potions as part of their schooling? Can a person who learns they've ingested a love potion steel themselves to resist its effects, just as someone can employ Occlumency while under the influence of Veritaserum? Given that love potions rob an individual of their autonomy, shouldn't these be as forbidden (or in wizard parlance, Unforgivable) as the Imperius Curse?

One worst-case scenario of love potions wreaking havoc on unsuspecting victims resulted in the birth of the most infamous Dark wizard of all time. During Harry's sixth year at Hogwarts, Dumbledore confides in Harry that he believes Merope Gaunt used a love potion to get Tom Riddle, Sr., to marry her, a union that produced the child who would grow up to be Lord Voldemort. If this is true, Merope would've had to continually administer the potion to her husband, a process by which she would have been "enslaving him by magical means," according to Dumbledore. Had Dumbledore managed to prove this assertion before his death, it's hard to say whether or not the Ministry of Magic would have moved to regulate or ban these problematic substances outright.

Transfiguration

Described by Professor Minerva McGonagall as "complex and dangerous magic," transfiguration is the act of altering an object's form or appearance by changing its molecular structure. Transfiguration can be applied to living and nonliving objects.

HISTORY OF TRANSFIGURATION COURSE

Transfiguration, a complex yet compulsory subject at Hogwarts, is governed by Gamp's Law of Elemental Transfiguration. It's likely one of the oldest subjects taught at the school since transfiguration forms a vital part of everyday magic. As one of the most difficult subjects a wizard can master, it requires a great deal of study and practice. Due to the nature of transfiguration, much can go wrong if the witch or wizard casting the spell doesn't understand what they're doing.

Young wizards learn transfiguration by mastering theoretical work they then put into practice. Students are introduced to various forms of transfiguration during their time at Hogwarts, which consist of transformation (changing an object into something else), untransfiguration (returning an object to its original state), switching (giving an object the characteristics of another), vanishment (making an object disappear) and conjuration (making objects appear out of thin air).

Students learn transformation in their first year. Their first class focuses on turning a match into a needle. This steadily advances until N.E.W.T. students eventually learn how to alter human appearances. One of their classes focuses on changing the color of their eyebrows as a means to practice this more difficult form of transfiguration. Switching spells are covered as part of students' fourth-year curriculum—in 1994, Hermione briefly considers such a spell while helping Harry prepare for the first task of the Triwizard Tournament, thinking he could perhaps switch the dragon's teeth for "wine gums." During students' fifth year, they are introduced to the fairly challenging magic of Vanishing Spells, which are tested during the O.W.L. exams. During students' sixth (and presumably seventh) year, they focus on conjuration, which is considered advanced magic.

NOTABLE TRANSFIGURATION PROFESSORS AND STUDENTS

Albus Dumbledore taught Transfiguration during Tom Riddle's time at Hogwarts. In 1956, **Minerva McGonagall** began teaching the subject alongside Dumbledore, and she continued to teach it after Dumbledore became headmaster. She still holds the role throughout **Harry**'s time at Hogwarts. It is not known who teaches the subject after McGonagall becomes headmistress in 1998.

Given Dumbledore's brilliant intellect, thoughtfulness and magical talent, he was likely an extraordinary professor. As Harry learns firsthand, Dumbledore's successor is a strict teacher who will not tolerate slackers in her class. McGonagall rarely lets students off the hook when it comes to homework or assignments. Failure to hand in Transfiguration homework results in detention, as **Draco Malfoy** discovers during the 1996–1997 school year. Professor McGonagall only accepts students with the best O.W.L. results into her N.E.W.T. class—scoring at least an E (Exceeds Expectations) is required.

There's no doubt Professor McGonagall possesses incredible knowledge and talent when it comes to the subject. During Harry's first lesson with her, she transforms her desk into a live pig to showcase the art of transfiguring to the class. This makes for a memorable visual, but an accomplished expert like McGonagall makes such spellwork look easy. When McGonagall has the first years turn matches into needles, they realize that this magic takes far more than a mere flick of the wrist to perform.

Hermione is one of the best students in her Transfiguration class. During her first Transfiguration lesson in the 1991–1992 academic year, she is the only student to make headway in the match-to-needle assignment. She continues to impress McGonagall during her time at Hogwarts, receiving an O (Outstanding) O.W.L. for the subject. Harry receives an E (Exceeds

Expectations) for Transfiguration, as does **Ron**, who continues with the subject in his sixth year.

REQUIRED TRANSFIGURATION TEXTBOOKS BY YEAR

A Beginner's Guide to Transfiguration by Emeric Switch is required reading for first-year students and includes everything they need to start learning the basics of Transfiguration. It is presumably used in their second year as well.

Intermediate Transfiguration (author unknown) is listed on third-year students' school supplies list and likely picks up where the previous book left off, teaching them more advanced forms of Transfiguration. This textbook likely also includes the theory students need in order to prepare for their O.W.L. exams.

A Guide to Advanced Transfiguration (author unknown) is listed on the sixth-year students' school supplies list. Its contents likely focus on very advanced Transfiguration concepts.

DESCRIPTION OF TRANSFIGURATION CLASSROOM

While the Transfiguration classroom's exact location is unknown, it's mentioned as being quite a distance from the Defense Against the Dark Arts professor's office located on the third floor.

The space consists of separate desks and a blackboard from which students often copy complicated notes. The teacher's desk is situated at the front and is likely decorated with a few candlesticks on it for late-night grading. Since students often practice transfiguration on creatures like beetles and raccoons, there are probably several cages either placed on shelves or hung from the ceiling. The classroom likely has windows, given the layouts of similar mandatory classes, and it's probably outfitted with several bookshelves. There might also be a chandelier or lanterns in neat rows along the walls to provide the room with sufficient light, especially on rainy days.

TRANSFIGURATIONS TAUGHT AT HOGWARTS

During Harry's time at Hogwarts, Professor McGonagall covers a wide range of transfigurations in her class.

FIRST YEAR

- **Match into Needle** At the end of the first lesson, only Hermione's match has changed in appearance; McGonagall shows the class how it had become silver and pointy.
- **Switching Spells** Hermione wins House points for Gryffindor for knowing about this type of magic.
- **Mouse into Snuffbox** During their end-of-term exam, students receive extra points for how well decorated and visually pleasing they can make their snuffbox. Points are deducted if it still sports whiskers.

SECOND YEAR

- **Beetle into Button**
- **Rabbits into Slippers** (see pg. 171)

THIRD YEAR

- **Teapot into Tortoise** After performing this transfiguration during an exam, students express concern about their tortoises having spouts for tails, breathing steam or having willow-patterned shells.

> In an example of transfiguration gone wrong, a student accidentally changes his friend into a badger during class.

FOURTH YEAR

- **Hedgehog into Pincushion** Presumably, it could be easier to transfigure one thing into another when they are similar in some way, including in shape. The idea is that the spiky spines on the back of a hedgehog are similar to pins on a pincushion.
- **Guinea Fowl into Guinea Pigs** It's presumably easier to transfigure one thing into another when they are similar in name.

- **Cross-Species Switches** Following the guinea fowl-into-guinea-pig lesson, McGonagall requires her fourth years to write an essay on how transfiguration spells have to be adapted for cross-species switches.

FIFTH YEAR

- **Vanishing Spells (starting with invertebrates before moving onto vertebrates) and Partial Vanishment** Although magic can differ significantly from science, transfiguration seems to abide by anatomical differences when it comes to difficulty. Students begin with creatures that have less-complex bodies (like snails) before moving on to creatures with more complex anatomy (like iguanas).

CONJURING SPELLS

- **Inanimatus Conjurus Spell** Although not explicitly explained, this spell likely involves the conjuring of inanimate objects.
- **Owl into Opera Glasses** The textbook *Intermediate Transfiguration* features a diagram of this process.

> Harry successfully makes an iguana vanish during the practical portion of his O.W.L. exam. In another transfiguration attempt, Hannah Abbott accidentally multiplies a ferret into a flock of flamingos.

SIXTH YEAR

- **Human Transfiguration** In preparation for the second task of the 1994–1995 Triwizard Tournament, Hermione laments that they won't learn human transfiguration until sixth year, otherwise Harry might consider transforming himself into a submarine to complete the task.

HISTORY OF ANIMAGI

An Animagus is a wizard who can transform into an animal. It is considered a different, more complex form of transfiguration than other human-to-animal transformations. The advanced magic involved in becoming an Animagus makes it an exceedingly rare skill, believed to be mastered by less than one out of every 1,000 wizards.

BECOMING AN ANIMAGUS

The process of becoming an Animagus is long and difficult, which foreshadows the many complex magical aspects involved in every transformation.

To become an Animagus, a wizard must keep a mandrake leaf in their mouth for an entire month. The leaf must then be removed and placed in a crystal phial under pure moon rays along with one of the wizard's hairs, a silver teaspoonful of dew untouched by sunlight or human feet for seven days and the chrysalis of a death's-head hawkmoth. The phial must be left in a quiet, dark, undisturbed place until the next electrical storm. While the phial is hidden, every dawn and dusk, the wizard must place their wand over their heart and speak the incantation "Amato Amino Animato Animagus." When lightning appears, the phial will have transformed into a potion that the wizard must drink. Only then will the first transformation into their Animagus form occur.

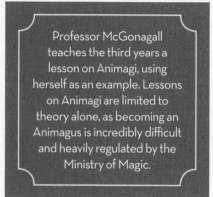

Professor McGonagall teaches the third years a lesson on Animagi, using herself as an example. Lessons on Animagi are limited to theory alone, as becoming an Animagus is incredibly difficult and heavily regulated by the Ministry of Magic.

This complex magic doesn't end after the wizard assumes their new form. Animagi fully retain their human brain (including thoughts, feelings and emotions, although they may be simplified) while transfigured. In addition, an Animagus's clothes remain with them but become invisible, absorbing into the skin as part of the process. An Animagus must be able to perform all of this complicated magic simultaneously. This level of difficulty likely contributes to why there are so few Animagi, although official numbers may be inaccurate due to the existence of unregistered individuals. In the 20th century, only seven Animagi are registered with the Ministry. However, Harry personally knows of at least four Animagi who are unregistered: James Potter, Sirius Black, Peter Pettigrew and Rita Skeeter.

GAMP'S LAW OF ELEMENTAL TRANSFIGURATION

Although the name may be confusing, Gamp's Law is not a legal rule put in place by the Ministry of Magic; instead, it is a "law" of science, much like Muggle scientist Isaac Newton's laws of motion. In the same way Newton discovered that an object at rest will stay at rest, Gamp discovered that the magic of transfiguration abides by certain conditions.

Gamp's Law of Elemental Transfiguration is not known, but it seems likely to be similar to the law of conservation of mass, which states that matter can be neither created nor destroyed but can be recombined in different forms. Gamp's Law may state that anything can be transfigured, conjured or vanished by combining substances in different forms. **There are five Principal Exceptions to Gamp's law, only one of which is known:**

FOOD CANNOT BE CREATED, IT MUST BE SUMMONED

According to Hermione, this is the first of the five Principal Exceptions to Gamp's Law. Food cannot be created from nothing.

Food can be:
- Summoned (so long as the summoner knows where it is)
- Transformed
- Multiplied

After Harry and Ron crash-land the Ford Anglia at Hogwarts in 1992, McGonagall provides them with a "refilling" platter of sandwiches. Although it may initially appear that she created the food out of thin air, Gamp's Law dictates she must be summoning the sandwiches from the Hogwarts kitchens.

When Dumbledore's Army finds refuge in the Room of Requirement during the Second Wizarding War, the room provides them with every necessity except food. Although it is not clear what level of magic or sentience the room possesses, the space is not exempt from Gamp's

Law. It would appear the room is incapable of summoning food from the Hogwarts kitchens. Instead, it provides safe passage to a different source of food at the Hog's Head Inn.

Unlike food, drinking water can be transfigured from nothing, although it could be argued that the water vapor always present in the atmosphere is the source of this transfiguration.

UNTRANSFIGURATION
Untransfiguration is the process of reversing transfiguration, returning an object or creature to its natural state.

KNOWN USES
- In *A Beginner's Guide to Transfiguration*, author Emeric Switch suggests using the Untranfiguration Spell to reverse transfigurations that have gone awry.
- Remus Lupin and Sirius Black likely use untransfiguration to transform Peter Pettigrew out of his Animagus form. When they perform the magic, it creates a "flash of blue-white light" from their wands. They perform this spell against Pettigrew's will, implying that the desire of the wizard performing the magic outweighs the desire of the living creature on which the magic is being performed. Interestingly, this logic is similar to that of the Room of Requirement, which always prioritizes the desires of the wizard currently using it if another wizard attempts to use it at the same time.

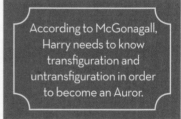

According to McGonagall, Harry needs to know transfiguration and untransfiguration in order to become an Auror.

- When Draco Malfoy is transfigured into a white ferret by Professor Moody (Barty Crouch, Jr., in disguise), McGonagall untransfigures him back into human form.

TRANSFIGURATION AND SENTIENCE

The magic of transfiguration raises serious ethical and moral questions concerning the welfare of the living creatures involved.

CREATURES INTO OBJECTS

Students are often asked to transfigure living creatures into objects during class or practical exams. In his second year, Harry and his classmates are asked to turn rabbits into slippers. If we assume these rabbits are living creatures, how does this type of magic affect their well-being? Does this cause the rabbits pain? Are they aware of what's happening? If so, are they traumatized? If not, what happens to their consciousness while they're in the transformed state? It's possible the rabbits are fully conscious but paralyzed while transformed, or they're magically anesthetized, which prevents them from experiencing or remembering any part of their time as slippers.

OBJECTS INTO CREATURES

Alternatively, students are often asked to transfigure objects into living creatures. In his third year, Harry and his classmates are tasked with turning teapots into tortoises. This magic raises a similar, more philosophical series of questions: Are these creatures actually alive? If so, how can magic create life? If not, what type of existence does the creature experience, if any?

While it's impossible to know what limits exist for transfiguration, the fact that Hogwarts continues to teach this type of magic to students indicates knowing the entirety of Gamp's Law may help explain the "how" but wouldn't necessarily provide enough context to answer the more ethical and moral question of "why."

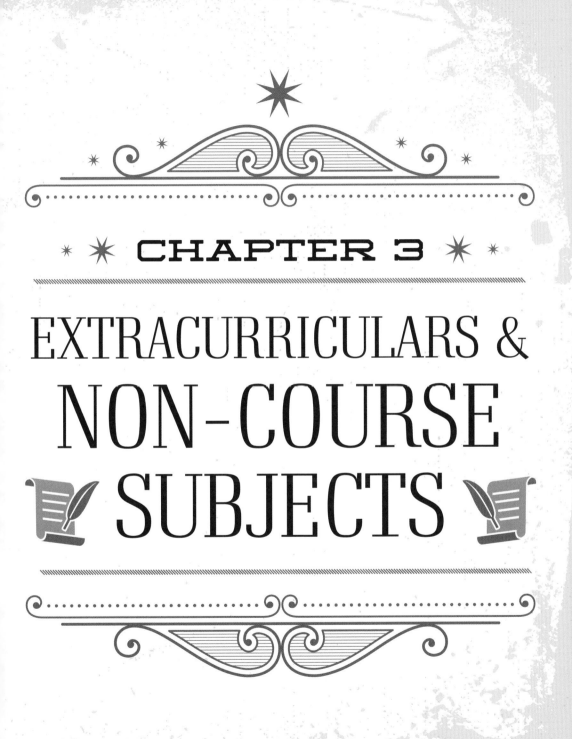

CHAPTER 3

EXTRACURRICULARS & NON-COURSE SUBJECTS

Extracurricular Activities

When the required coursework and studying aren't enough to fill Hogwarts students' free time, they have plenty of options for extracurricular activities. From organized clubs and seriously competitive teams to more casual interests and hobbies, there's more to life at Hogwarts than in-class instruction.

Quidditch is an enormously popular sport within the magical community, and even first years from non-wizarding upbringings can quickly develop an interest and learn the rules. It should be noted that while first-year students take compulsory flying lessons, they are not allowed to bring their own broomsticks to Hogwarts. Typically, beginning in their second year, students may choose to try out for their House's Quidditch team. Those who do not make the team or are not interested in the rigorous training and game schedules are free to use the Quidditch pitch when it's available to develop their skills or fly recreationally.

Each of the four Houses at Hogwarts has its own Quidditch team. These coed teams are made up of seven players of varying ages, with each position fielding different responsibilities on the pitch. The Gryffindor Quidditch team that wins the Quidditch Cup during the 1993–1994 school year is outlined on the table on page 176.

Each year, one player is named Quidditch captain, a title marked by a badge mailed with the school supplies list each summer. The captain schedules practices and determines who makes the team. Captains are typically fifth-, sixth- or seventh-year students who have experience on their respective teams. Some captains go on to pursue a professional Quidditch career after school—Oliver Wood, for example, joins Puddlemere United.

Students who do not make the final cut at tryouts early in the school year may yet get their chance to participate in an organized game later on. Given that Quidditch is so dangerous (injuries can result in a student losing consciousness or requiring an extended stay in the hospital wing), it is imperative that captains be prepared to call on a reserve player to take the place of an indisposed athlete.

Team members can also be prohibited from playing in a single game before it starts. In some cases, the student has earned a detention that was scheduled during a match. Captains and/or teachers may decide to remove a player from a match for one reason or another, such as poor sportsmanship. Students can also earn a blanket ban for the year or indefinitely as punishment from strict teachers. During the 1995–1996 school year, Dolores Umbridge places a lifelong Quidditch ban upon Harry and George Weasley as punishment for physically attacking a member of the Slytherin team who'd been hurling nasty insults at Gryffindor players.

Each year, six Quidditch games are held so that each team gets the chance to play a single match against each of its three opposing teams. The team that accrues the most points by the final match of the school year wins the Quidditch Cup, a massive silver trophy. The winning team also earns a generous number of points for their House, often a significant factor in deciding who will take home the House Cup.

Below is an example of a typical schedule of games during the school year:

MATCH	PAIRING	TIMING
1	Gryffindor vs. Slytherin	Early November
2	Hufflepuff vs. Ravenclaw	Late November or early December
3	Ravenclaw vs. Slytherin	January
4	Gryffindor vs. Hufflepuff	Late February or early March
5	Hufflepuff vs. Slytherin	Late March or early April
6	Gryffindor vs. Ravenclaw	Late May or early June

TEAM POSITION	DESCRIPTION	PLAYER NAME	PLAYER YEAR
1 Keeper	Protects the three goalposts from the other team's Chasers	Oliver Wood (Captain)	Seventh
3 Chasers	Handle the Quaffle, which they attempt to toss through the opposing team's goalposts	Angelina Johnson	Fifth
		Alicia Spinnet	Fifth
		Katie Bell	Fourth
2 Beaters	Use bats to knock Bludgers at the opposing team's players	Fred Weasley	Fifth
		George Weasley	Fifth
1 Seeker	Searches for and attempts to catch the Golden Snitch	Harry Potter	Third

Games are highly anticipated events, with the majority of faculty, staff and students attending. Some students also enjoy watching tryouts and practices. Another way students can get involved is to volunteer as a Quidditch commentator. Notable commentators include Lee Jordan and Luna Lovegood.

Another (though decidedly less popular) extracurricular available to Hogwarts students is the **Gobstones Club**. Gobstones is an ancient wizarding game that resembles the Muggle game of marbles. A set of 30 Gobstones is divided up so that two opposing players start with 15 stones each. A magical element to Gobstones is that the stones squirt a putrid-smelling liquid into a player's face each time they lose a point. Gobstones are typically made of stone, though an expensive, flashy set may be made of precious metals such as solid gold.

Younger Hogwarts students tend to be more interested in Gobstones than older ones, who may "grow out" of the hobby. Though the game's popularity doesn't rival that of Quidditch, devoted players can advance to professional competitions after leaving school. There are national leagues, such as the National Gobstone Association, as well as international tournaments.

The title Captain of the Hogwarts Gobstones Team is granted to a student each year. One holder of this title is Eileen Prince, mother of Professor Severus Snape.

Various clubs are dedicated to special academic pursuits, such as **Charms Club**. It is likely students form similar groups for other subjects, such as Potions, Alchemy and Astronomy, or particular interests such as healing or music. Students can form small study groups, and this may be particularly useful for older students preparing for O.W.L. and N.E.W.T. examinations.

In fall 1992, Defense Against the Dark Arts professor Gilderoy Lockhart establishes a **Dueling Club** so that students have the chance to practice combat in a safe and controlled environment. Its first and only meeting had rather disastrous results. It was during this meeting that the school discovered Harry was a Parselmouth, which led many to suspect he was the Heir of Slytherin purported to have opened the Chamber of Secrets. However, a positive effect of this meeting was Harry first learning the Disarming Charm, a simple yet effective spell that he would go on to use many times against Lord Voldemort. The Dueling Club does not meet again during this year, and it is unknown whether the club is brought back in subsequent years.

Outside of school-sanctioned activities, Hogwarts students may occasionally challenge each other to a duel. In these cases, it is customary for each side to choose a second, though it is not expected that students would either attempt or actually be able to kill each other.

During the 1995-1996 school year, Umbridge's poor instruction on Defense Against the Dark Arts compels many students concerned about the unacknowledged rise of Voldemort to form their own defense association: **Dumbledore's Army,** a group that regularly meets in secret within the Room of Requirement. Owing to his extensive experience confronting the Dark Arts, Harry leads his fellow students in practicing defensive as well as offensive magic that he has found useful in real-world scenarios.

The meetings are well-liked by most participants despite the risk of detention or worse, given that it defies the Hogwarts High Inquisitor's recent ban on all clubs, teams and gatherings. Since the club is forced to keep its existence a secret, special fake Galleons are enchanted to communicate meeting dates and times to members. Armed with their new skills and knowledge of defensive magic, many members of the D.A. go on to perform well on their exams (as well as defend themselves against antagonistic students). The organization breaks up after Voldemort is publicly revealed to have returned to power but reconvenes in secret when Snape becomes headmaster in 1997. Several D.A. members later fight in the Battle of Hogwarts.

After Dumbledore's Army is founded, Umbridge forms the **Inquisitorial Squad.** This select group of students is tasked with serving her agenda (which, by extension, is the Ministry of Magic's agenda), policing the corridors for anyone defying her Educational Decrees. The squad also makes a point of eavesdropping on conversations, checking to see if anyone is discussing Voldemort's return—such individuals are reported. All the students in the squad are Slytherins, including Draco Malfoy, Vincent Crabbe and Gregory Goyle. To the relief of many students (and likely staff), the Inquisitorial Squad is short-lived, as it is corrupt and answers only to Umbridge.

A long-standing and honorable legacy at Hogwarts is the privilege of being named **prefect**. This title is traditionally awarded to two fifth-year students from each Hogwarts House at the start of each year. Prefects tend to be responsible students who possess good leadership skills. These students must attend a meeting on their yearly train ride to Hogwarts to hear about their duties, which involve shepherding first years around the school, patrolling corridors and watching out for poor behavior such as bullying or being out after curfew.

Prefects remain in their role into sixth and seventh year so that each House has six prefects at once. Each year, a Head Boy and Head Girl from seventh year are also named, and these are typically standout prefects.

Below is a list of notable prefects, Head Boys and Head Girls.

- **Albus Dumbledore,** *Gryffindor Prefect and Head Boy*
- **Minerva McGonagall,** *Gryffindor Prefect and Head Girl*
- **Tom Riddle,** *Slytherin Prefect and Head Boy*
- **Remus Lupin,** *Gryffindor Prefect*
- **James Potter,** *Head Boy*
- **Lily Evans,** *Gryffindor Prefect (likely) and Head Girl*
- **Bill Weasley,** *Gryffindor Prefect and Head Boy*
- **Charlie Weasley,** *Gryffindor Prefect*
- **Percy Weasley,** *Gryffindor Prefect and Head Boy*
- **Penelope Clearwater,** *Ravenclaw Prefect*
- **Cedric Diggory,** *Hufflepuff Prefect*
- **Hermione Granger,** *Gryffindor Prefect*
- **Draco Malfoy,** *Slytherin Prefect*
- **Pansy Parkinson,** *Slytherin Prefect*
- **Ron Weasley,** *Gryffindor Prefect*

Prefects, Quidditch captains, Head Boys and Head Girls are all identifiable by the badges pinned to their robes. As a perk, they may use the special, password-protected prefects' bathroom located on the fifth floor of the castle. The white, marble-clad room features a marvelous chandelier and a swimming pool-sized sunken tub with various taps for a magical and luxurious bathing experience.

The **Slug Club** is a group of esteemed students handpicked by Professor Horace Slughorn. Founded during Slughorn's first stint at the school, the group is later revived during the 1996–1997 school year when he comes out of retirement to assume the post of Potions Master. Members are students who have great connections to prominent

CONTINUED ON PAGE 181

NOTABLE MEMBERS OF THE SLUG CLUB

STUDENT	NOTES
Tom Riddle	Used flattery and charm to manipulate Slughorn into providing him with information on Horcruxes
Barnabas Cuffe	Editor of the *Daily Prophet* by 1996; accepts Slughorn's input on daily news
Dirk Cresswell	Head of the Goblin Liaison Office for the Ministry of Magic; provided Slughorn with exclusive insight on Gringotts Bank
Gwenog Jones	Captain of the Holyhead Harpies Quidditch team
Lily Evans	Particularly gifted in Potions; murdered by Voldemort
Regulus Black (likely)	Slytherin Seeker; an heir to the Black family fortune; a Death Eater who later betrayed Voldemort; killed by Inferi
Blaise Zabini	His mother was a witch famous for her beauty and connected to the mysterious deaths of at least seven wealthy husbands.
Cormac McLaggen	Nephew of his Uncle Tiberius, a well-connected Ministry of Magic employee
Ginny Weasley	Impresses Slughorn with her expert use of the Bat-Bogey Hex
Harry Potter	Famous for surviving Voldemort's Killing Curse as a baby, winning the Triwizard Tournament, etc.
Hermione Granger	Demonstrates her strong academic prowess by answering questions in the very first Potions lesson
Marcus Belby*	Nephew of Damocles, inventor of the Wolfsbane Potion and recipient of the Order of Merlin
Melinda Bobbin	Member of a family that owns a large chain of apothecaries
Neville Longbottom*	Son of Aurors Frank and Alice Longbottom, who were tortured into insanity by Death Eaters

*only present at first meeting

witches and wizards, show exceptional academic and magical abilities or are expected to have illustrious careers and/or followings in the magical community. Ex-members who remain on good terms with Slughorn may be given introductions to further their success, and these individuals often reward their old professor in whatever ways they can.

Professor Slughorn tends to hold parties exclusive to Slug Club members and, occasionally, their plus ones. Prominent ex-members and otherwise interesting people can also be invited; at Slughorn's 1996 Christmas party, even a vampire named Sanguini is in attendance. Though some students may be invited to attend Slug Club events early in the year, these gatherings may give Slughorn the opportunity to get to know them better and weed out those who show little promise for fame or connections, such as Marcus Belby, who was not on close terms with his well-known uncle Damocles.

Social justice-minded students might decide to launch a philanthropic organization within Hogwarts. Hermione is one example: Upon witnessing the poor treatment of Barty Crouch's house-elf, Winky, following the Death Eater attack at the 1994 Quidditch World Cup, she launches the **Society for the Promotion of Elfish Welfare (aka S.P.E.W.)** in an effort to inform her fellow Hogwarts students on house-elf enslavement and rights. After naming Ron treasurer and Harry secretary, she manages to recruit students (e.g., Neville Longbottom) to join for the cost of two Sickles. Hermione leaves hand-knit wool hats around the Gryffindor common room for Hogwarts house-elves to find in the hopes that they might set these elves free from servitude; unfortunately, the insulted elves avoid their obligatory cleaning of Gryffindor Tower so that only Dobby, the free elf, would do this cleaning and wear the hats. Despite Hermione's efforts, the group never gains traction.

Hogwarts lacks a **drama club** by the time Harry begins his schooling, but decades prior at some point during Dumbledore's tenure as a Transfiguration professor, students attempted to put on a play based on "The Fountain of Fair Fortune" during Christmastime. The performance was conceptualized by then-Herbology professor Herbert Beery, a lover of dramatic arts. Other staff members of the day contributed: Dumbledore managed special effects, and Care of Magical Creatures professor Silvanus Kettleburn provided a fiery, magically enlarged Ashwinder to stand in as the gigantic worm.

Unfortunately for everyone involved, Beery failed to account for the adverse effects of youthful emotions running high in a dramatic environment. A sudden breakup of the students playing Amata and Sir Luckless just before the performance led to the actors altering the plot and ultimately attacking each other mid-act. To make matters worse, the "worm" combusted, causing the set to erupt into flames and forcing everyone to evacuate the Great Hall. As a cautionary measure, Headmaster Armando Dippet banned any repeat attempts to stage the play, a prohibition no headmaster has since lifted.

OTHER ACTIVITIES

Apart from clubs, teams and organizations, Hogwarts students enjoy a variety of hobbies and pastimes. **Wizard chess**, in which the chess pieces come alive and fight according to the player's orders, is a popular game among students (or at least more popular than Gobstones). Some students play **Exploding Snap**, while others are heavily interested in collecting the trading cards packaged with Chocolate Frogs. Beginning in their third year, students can kill time shopping in Hogsmeade on certain weekends, as the nearby wizarding village is within walking distance of the school. Depending on their interests, students might choose to pursue artistic talents (Dean Thomas), photography (Colin Creevey), caring for plants (Neville Longbottom) or experimenting with magical pranks (Fred and George Weasley).

Non-Course Subjects

There's plenty to learn about the intricacies of magic, so it's no surprise some of it doesn't fit neatly into a one-size-fits-all curriculum at Hogwarts.

APPARITION

WHAT IT IS

Apparition is magic that allows the user to "teleport" from one place to another. A person who uses this spell will disappear from where they are and reappear at their desired destination almost instantaneously.

In Britain, the Ministry of Magic requires wizards to obtain a license to Apparate. This both ensures that a wizard can safely perform the magic and helps prevent criminal activity against Muggles.

> Although house-elves can Apparate, they are likely not required to be licensed because of their perceived inferiority in wizarding society. Similarly, certain magical beasts, including the phoenix and the Diricawl, can Apparate—apparently doing so without Ministry regulation.

In locations used by wizards, enchantments can be placed to prevent Apparition directly into the area. An Anti-Disapparition Jinx can be placed to prevent anyone from Apparating away (otherwise known as Disapparating). Places like the Ministry of Magic, Hogwarts grounds and Azkaban prison have these enchantments on them.

HOW IT WORKS

Apparition is complex magic and young wizards are encouraged to take lessons before applying for their license. Hogwarts students are offered the option to take a course in Apparition taught by an official from the Ministry of Magic.

Though convenient, Apparition can be loud and uncomfortable. The act can create a jarring, popping noise similar to a car backfiring and, according to Harry Potter, feels like being "forced through a very tight rubber tube."

While not a formal class at Hogwarts, Apparition training sessions are offered to students who are 17 years old or will be turning 17 by the end of the following summer. In 1997, the 12-week course costs 12 Galleons and is taught by Wilkie Twycross, a Ministry of Magic employee. The course is held in the Great Hall, allowing students to spread out in the space. During the hour-long lessons, the Anti-Apparition Charm that prevents anyone from Apparating within Hogwarts walls is temporarily lifted. Under the careful supervision of the instructor, students practice disappearing and reappearing inside a hoop placed on the floor in front of them. At the end of the training course, students who have turned 17 can take a licensure examination. Students who splinch (see below) during the exam automatically fail the test and have to retake it, regardless of the severity of their error. Prior to the exam, additional practice sessions are offered in Hogsmeade under strict supervision.

THE THREE D'S

Wilkie Twycross explains that Apparition involves the three d's: destination, determination and deliberation. While Apparating, wizards must be "determined" to reach their "destination" by moving with "deliberation."

LIMITATIONS

The difficulty of Apparition increases as the distance to one's desired destination increases. Should a wizard attempt Apparating across great distances (like intercontinental travel), they are at an increased risk of injury.

A contributing factor is the fact that Apparition is considerably easier if a wizard can vividly visualize their destination.

Although this form of transportation is the most convenient of all magical options, it is difficult to master and can have disastrous consequences if performed incorrectly.

SPLINCHING

Splinching is the "separation of random body parts" that can occur if a wizard is not properly focused during Apparition. The severity ranges from something as minor as losing eyebrow hair to life-threatening injuries.

In 1994, Arthur Weasley tells Harry and Hermione a story about two wizards who attempted to Apparate without a license and ended up splinching themselves in half.

During her first Apparition lesson in 1996, Susan Bones splinches herself, detaching her leg from her body. Luckily, the adults present were able to quickly reattach it.

SIDE-ALONG APPARITION

A wizard can transport more than one person via Apparition. This is particularly useful if traveling with underage wizards or unlicensed adults.

To do this, the individuals traveling together must hold on to one another tightly—the Ministry recommends holding on to an arm—while performing the magic.

If all individuals know how to Apparate, they do not need to hold on as tightly. This is because the main Apparator is guiding them along to the destination rather than fully transporting them.

A person can be forcibly Apparated; because of the physical aspects involved, it is extremely difficult or impossible to break free.

THE TRACE

It is not only lack of training that prevents young wizards from Apparating. Legally, underage wizards are not allowed to perform magic outside of school. If wizards under 17 do perform magic, the Improper Use of Magic Office is alerted under the requirements set forth by the Decree for the Reasonable Restriction of Underage Sorcery, which was written in 1875.

To track this, the Ministry of Magic uses the Trace, which allows them to track all magical activity performed by or around underage wizards. This is an almost impossible task if the underage person comes from a wizarding family, as magic would be used almost constantly by the adults in their household. The Trace is most likely meant to monitor Muggle-born wizards or any underage wizards in predominantly Muggle areas.

What magic is behind the Trace is largely unknown, but it may be related to the magic behind Apparition. The two are similar in their focus on location and ability to be regulated by the Ministry.

OCCLUMENCY

WHAT IT IS

Occlumency is the practice of magically closing the mind to prevent individuals from seeing thoughts, memories or other personal information you don't want them to see. An individual accomplished in the art of Occlumency is known as an Occlumens.

HOW IT WORKS

To protect one's mind from intrusion, one must endeavor to clear it of any emotion or thought. Memories are only discovered when an emotion tied to that memory lingers in the mind. Having a blank, calm mind is the end goal in that nothing is readily seen or noticed.

It is not enough, however, to simply wipe the mind once and be done with the matter: Occlumency requires constantly keeping your shields up and maintaining focus, which can only be accomplished by remaining in control. Not allowing emotions or thoughts to leak into your mind takes a great deal of discipline and willpower to maintain. If you lose control, the attacker can immediately take advantage, using a single memory or thought to push further into your mind.

While maintaining control of your mind, it is important to distract or disarm the person attempting to penetrate it. This can be done by casting the Disarming Charm. This solution will only work if the individual attempting to enter your mind needs a wand to do so. A gifted Legilimens does not require a wand, so it is important to distract them by breaking their concentration.

Another way to break the attacker's concentration is by casting a jinx or hex, such as when Harry produces a Stinging Hex during his first Occlumency lesson with Professor Snape. That case, however, is an unintentional magical outburst due to losing control. While this can distract the attacker, it is better to remain in control of your mind and the situation at hand and use the Disarming Charm.

You can also cast a Shield Charm, which may result in a rebounding effect, allowing you to push into your attacker's mind. This also happens between Harry and Snape during their Occlumency lessons. It cannot really be called Legilimency, though, since it is not an intentional, conscious effort to enter the mind.

Once you have mastered clearing your mind completely, you can move on to clearing the thoughts or emotions related to particular memories you're trying to hide instead. This will give your attacker a false sense of success because they can still see into your mind, but only what you allow them to see, giving you more control of the situation. This can cause them to believe you are being truthful and not further pry into your mind.

Occlumency can only be actively used while you are awake, meaning your mind is only protected in sleep if you practice the skill effectively before bed. Harry is advised to do this to protect his mind from Voldemort but does not do so.

LIMITATIONS

If you do not practice Occlumency before bed, your mind could be unguarded while you sleep. This can allow anyone to see what you previously hid from them or implant false memories or dreams. Additionally, even a skilled Occlumens can fall prey to a mental attack when feeling intense emotions like anger or excitement. It's during these emotions that it is most difficult to protect your mind because it is poring over thoughts related to them. Learning how to control not only your mind but also your strong emotions ensures your mind is protected even when experiencing them.

LESSONS AT HOGWARTS

Students may receive private lessons from professors on the subject (in Harry's case, whether they'd like to or not). During the 1995–1996 school year, Harry's weekly Occlumency lessons with Snape begin at Dumbledore's request. The headmaster hopes this will teach Harry to protect his mind from Voldemort, especially after Voldemort becomes aware of the connection between himself and the teen.

NOTABLE OCCLUMENS

Barty Crouch, Jr., is likely an Occlumens to some extent, in that he was able to conceal his true identity throughout the school year. It's hard to tell whether Polyjuice Potion alone could achieve a ruse of that considerable duration.

Albus Dumbledore is a self-described Occlumens. When explaining to Harry why he opted for Snape to teach him the practice, he notes he could've taught Harry himself but had worried Voldemort would exploit that link.

Bellatrix Lestrange teaches Occlumency to her nephew, Draco, suggesting she is a skilled Occlumens. She keeps several secrets from others, including the location of Helga Hufflepuff's cup and her knowledge of the Unbreakable Vow she witnesses between Snape and her sister, Narcissa Malfoy.

Draco Malfoy is a "very gifted" Occlumens, likely due to his ability to compartmentalize his feelings. He uses these skills during Harry's sixth year to prevent anyone from learning of his mission on behalf of Lord Voldemort, which includes keeping his involvement in the cursing of Katie Bell from Snape.

Severus Snape is a highly accomplished Occlumens. Hiding large portions of his mind from Lord Voldemort proves critical to his success as a spy. It's no wonder, then, that Dumbledore selects him to teach Occlumency to Harry. Ultimately, Voldemort never discovers from Snape that he has long been a double agent.

Lord Voldemort is able to hide his actions at Hogwarts from Professor Albus Dumbledore, a known Legilimens. While a student, he successfully conceals his involvement with the Chamber of Secrets and his actions toward his late family. The summer between Harry's fifth and sixth years at Hogwarts, Dumbledore comments that he believes Voldemort is utilizing Occlumency to close the connection Harry has with him.

LEGILIMENCY

WHAT IT IS

Legilimency is the art of magically entering someone's mind, typically with the intention of finding out information of which they wouldn't otherwise be cognizant. This could include memories, emotions or general thoughts. It entails piercing through the layers in someone's mind, peeling them back like an onion and trying to understand the thoughts rather than simply read them. An individual accomplished in the art of Legilimency is called a Legilimens.

HOW IT WORKS

To enter another's mind, one can wave their own wand and utter the incantation *Legilimens*. The person attempting to use Legilimency should be close to the person on which they are trying to use it. A highly skilled Legilimens can complete the spell nonverbally and without the use of a wand. Some, like Voldemort, can even do it from afar (though this may owe to his preexisting connection with Harry).

A Legilimens may not always enter a mind with the goal of finding something—they may enter with the intention to plant a false memory. This happens in Harry's fifth year when Voldemort implants a vision of Sirius being tortured at the Ministry of Magic in Harry's mind.

There are rare occurrences in which individuals are born with the ability. Queenie Goldstein, an American witch who attended Ilvermorny, is an example of this: She need only look at someone to see what is in their mind, never needing her wand or an incantation. Her level of skill is not something that can be taught.

LESSONS AT HOGWARTS

Legilimency is not formally taught at Hogwarts, though students may receive private lessons. It is more likely that students learn and practice this skill outside of Hogwarts with the help of family members or private tutors. It is not known if there are any students taking lessons in Legilimency during Harry's time at Hogwarts.

NOTABLE LEGILIMENS

Albus Dumbledore is a self-described Legilimens, which he explains as the ability to know when he's being lied to.

Severus Snape is skilled in the art of Legilimency, able to enter Harry's mind to help him practice the art of Occlumency. However, he is more skilled in the art of concealing his own mind than he is at entering someone else's.

Lord Voldemort is a skilled Legilimens, not needing an incantation or wand to enter someone's mind. He can use the ability from afar, implanting fake information in Harry's mind as bait to lure Harry into a trap. Despite his skill, he never appears to thwart Snape's Occlumency.

The Sorting Hat, used to Sort Hogwarts students into one of four Houses, was given the power of Legilimency by the four founders of the school with the intent of selecting students to join their House according to their traits and desires. It is unclear if students trained in Occlumency can prevent the hat from entering their minds.

MAGICAL MEDICINE

Magical medicine is a highly useful subject and a known career path in the wizarding community. While there is no designated medicine or healing class offered at Hogwarts, students learn various healing practices across the school's core curriculum.

In order to pursue a career as a Healer, students need to achieve either "Outstanding" or "Exceeds Expectations" on the N.E.W.T. examinations in Charms, Herbology, Defense Against the Dark Arts, Potions and Transfiguration. Elements of healing magic can be acquired through each of those classes.

During Charms lessons, students learn useful everyday spells, including some that can be employed in medical situations. *Episkey* is the incantation for a charm used to heal minor injuries such as broken noses and split lips. *Anapneo* is the incantation to clear the throat of someone who is choking. It is not known during what year of school students learn these charms.

In Herbology class, students are taught about various plants with healing properties. For example, dittany is used to heal wounds, and dried nettles are an ingredient in a potion that cures boils. In their second year, Herbology students learn how to handle and care for mandrakes, whose roots are used to revive Petrified individuals.

Students learn how to cast Stunning Spells in Defense Against the Dark Arts class. Presumably, they are also taught how to cast the counterspell that revives a stunned individual. It is likely that the counterspell Rennervate is taught to students in their fourth year at Hogwarts. Harry practices stunning Ron in preparation for the Triwizard Tournament and would need to know how to revive him after successfully casting the Stunning Spell. Harry also uses this counterspell to revive Dumbledore after the latter drinks Voldemort's cursed potion in 1997, meaning Harry knew how to cast the spell by his sixth year at school.

In Potions class, students learn how to brew antidotes to poisons. There are also potions that address medical situations, such as the Pepperup Potion used by Madam Pomfrey to cure a wave of sickness that sweeps through the school during the 1992–1993 school year.

Transfiguration may be a useful subject for a Healer to master, as objects can be transfigured into surgical supplies. The Vanishing Spell, which is taught in Transfiguration classes, can also be used to clean up blood and other bodily fluids in a medical setting.

Upon graduating from Hogwarts, students will have acquired at least some knowledge of the art of healing. Those who wish to pursue a career as a Healer undergo additional training after leaving school.

Madam Pomfrey, a prime example of someone skilled in healing magic, tends to injured and ill students and staff in the Hogwarts hospital wing. On rare occasions, students and staff are transferred to St. Mungo's Hospital for Magical Maladies and Injuries for intensive care. In 1996, after touching a cursed necklace that had been intended to be delivered to Albus Dumbledore, Katie Bell is sent to St Mungo's.

St. Mungo's Healers are known to treat magical illnesses such as spattergroit and dragon pox, as well as injuries. Healers at St. Mungo's wear a uniform of lime-green robes with a wand-and-bone logo stitched on the chest.

Mediwizards are another example of a job in magical medicine. These wizards are seen tending to an injured Quidditch player on the pitch at the 1994 Quidditch World Cup. It is unclear if mediwizards are the wizarding equivalent of paramedics and first responders or if they are the same as Healers, brought on site to deal with incidents outside of a hospital setting.

EXCHANGE PROGRAMS

Exchange programs exist in the wizarding community, giving students the opportunity to experience differing educations and cultures. The Brazilian wizarding school, Castelobruxo, is known to have offered a program popular with European students who wish to study magical plants and creatures native to South America, provided students pay their own way. Bill Weasley was invited on such a trip by his Brazilian pen pal, but since his parents couldn't afford the cost, he couldn't go. When Bill was forced to decline the invitation, his pen pal became offended and sent Bill a cursed hat that made his ears shrivel up.

Hogwarts also returns the favor and hosts members of other wizarding schools. Former Castelobruxo Headmistress Benedita Dourado is known to have visited Hogwarts on at least one occasion as part of these exchange trips.

The Triwizard Tournament is another opportunity for students of various schools to study abroad. During the 1994–1995 school year, students from Beauxbatons and Durmstrang visit Hogwarts for an extended period of time while the chosen champions compete.

Students from the visiting schools do not sleep in Hogwarts dormitories during their stay, however: The Beauxbatons delegation stays in the enormous carriage that transported them from France to Scotland, while the Durmstrang students bunk on the ship on which they sailed to Hogwarts.

Advanced, Taboo & Forbidden Magic

The Ministry of Magic has various laws in place that govern the use of magic. Some of these ensure that the magical community stays hidden from Muggles while others forbid witches and wizards from practicing Dark magic freely. Naturally, these laws extend to the students at Hogwarts and largely shape what they are allowed to learn at school.

SPELL CREATION

Wizards who possess great magical abilities have the power to create new spells. Through an unknown process, magic can be harnessed through wand movements, incantations and nonverbal intentions to produce the desired outcome.

Although the process requires immense knowledge and skill, there have been multiple examples of young wizards successfully creating new spells. Fred and George Weasley, Tom Riddle and Severus Snape all mastered the art of spell creation before (or soon after) leaving Hogwarts.

KNOWN SPELL INVENTORS

ALBUS DUMBLEDORE

Patronus Charm Communication
Although it is unknown when Dumbledore invented this modified use of the Patronus Charm, it was particularly useful during the Second Wizarding War.

HERPO THE FOUL
Horcrux
The creation of a Horcrux involves splitting one's soul and encapsulating it in an object. The process surrounding the making of a Horcrux is unknown, but it does involve murder. Herpo was the first wizard to create a Horcrux; he likely invented the process. Because of this and his creation of the basilisk, he is considered one of the most notorious practitioners of the Dark Arts.

BASIL HORTON AND RANDOLPH KEITCH
Horton-Keitch Braking Charm
Applied to all broomsticks manufactured by the Comet Trading Company, this charm allows for more precise stopping while riding a broom. Horton and Keitch invented the charm to help Quidditch players avoid overshooting goals or flying off the pitch.

GILDEROY LOCKHART
Face in the Sky
This spell casts a glowing, holographic image of Lockhart's face in the sky. Lockhart invented this spell during his time as a student at Hogwarts; the incantation is unknown. The spell creates an effect incredibly similar to *Morsmordre*, which Voldemort and the Death Eaters use to cast the Dark Mark over the homes of their victims. Although all-around distasteful, Lockhart's creation of this spell is unsurprising considering his reputation.

MERWYN THE MALICIOUS
Unpleasant Jinxes and Hexes
Although it is unclear which particular spells Merwyn invented, he is infamous in the wizarding world for creating many in his time practicing the Dark Arts. Merwyn, like many other famous wizards throughout history, appears on Chocolate Frog cards.

DAISY PENNIFOLD
Slowing Charm (possibly)
This spell causes its intended target to descend more slowly than it would naturally. Although it's unknown whether or not Pennifold invented the charm herself, she is well-known for having used it in 1711 to make catching the Quaffle easier and safer for Chasers during Quidditch matches. These Quaffles are known as Pennifold Quaffles and are still commonly used.

URQUHART RACKHARROW
Entrail-Expelling Curse
This spell was invented in the 1600s by Rackharrow. Given his portrait hangs in St. Mungo's, the spell is likely a medical treatment that expels the contents of entrails rather than entrails themselves.

Because creating new spells requires a considerable amount of talent and knowledge, it is a dangerous process. According to Luna Lovegood, her mother Pandora was very talented when it came to experimenting with spells. Despite her ability, one of Pandora's experiments turned disastrous and resulted in the witch losing her life.

MNEMONE RADFORD
Memory Modifying Charm
Also known as the Forgetfulness Charm, this spell's incantation is *Obliviate*. It is incredibly powerful and can be used to erase a person's memories. Not only did Radford create the spell, but she was also the British Ministry of Magic's first Obliviator, a position that involves modifying or erasing Muggles' memories to protect the International Statute of Secrecy and keep the wizarding world a secret.

TOM RIDDLE
Morsmordre
It is speculated this spell was created by Riddle, but there is no known confirmation. This spell enables those who cast it to display an image of the Dark Mark in the sky. During the First Wizarding War, the mark would be displayed over the homes of victims to instill fear.

Unsupported Flight
Throughout wizarding history, many have tried to create a spell that would enable flight without the support of a magical object (like a broomstick). At some point before or during the Second Wizarding War, Tom Riddle was able to do what no wizard had ever done before, succeeding in his quest to fly unaided by any object. Other than Voldemort himself, only two other wizards are known to have learned the ability: Snape, who was taught by Voldemort, and Voldemort's daughter, Delphini, who learns the magic on her own to honor her father.

Unspecified Resurrection Spells
In order to resurrect himself, Voldemort claims to have invented more than one spell. These spells are supposedly to assist in creating a new body for what remains of the his soul.

ELLIOT SMETHWYCK
Cushioning Charm
This spell, whose incantation is *Molliare*, creates a cushioning effect. It is often cast on broomsticks to make flying more comfortable.

SEVERUS SNAPE
Langlock
This jinx causes the tongue to stick to the roof of the mouth, preventing speech, and works on humans and poltergeists. Snape invented this spell and wrote it down in his Potions textbook alongside countless other notes.

Levicorpus
Particularly popular with Hogwarts students in the 1970s, this spell is often used as a practical joke. When cast, a person is lifted into the air by their ankle. Snape invented and recorded this spell in his Potions textbook in the same manner as his other inventions. The counterjinx to *Levicorpus* is *Liberacorpus*, which Snape also invented.

Muffliato
When cast, this spell creates an "unidentifiable buzzing sound" in the ears of anyone near the caster. This prevents eavesdropping and allows for private conversations in otherwise occupied spaces.

Sectumsempra
An incredibly violent curse with deadly consequences, this spell was created by Snape, who wrote the incantation in his Potions book and noted no other details besides that it was "for enemies." When cast, the curse slashes through the flesh of the target, creating deep lacerations and severe, life-threatening injuries. However, with Snape's level of finesse, it is also possible to control the severity of the attack and allow for a range of injuries, from minor to more severe.

Toenail-Growing Hex
This spell causes toenails to grow incredibly quickly. The incantation is unknown. Snape noted this hex in the margins of his Potions textbook.

FELIX SUMMERBEE
Cheering Charm
When affected by a Cheering Charm, a person feels delighted. Unfortunately, if performed incorrectly, the spell can cause unwanted fits of hysterical laughter. The charm is taught to third years in Charms class at Hogwarts and, in 1994, was part of Professor Flitwick's final exam.

FRED AND GEORGE WEASLEY
Weasleys' Wizard Wheezes
Fred and George create many practical joke products ranging from ailment-inducing candies to trick wands. The twins sell their inventions illicitly at Hogwarts, where they gain not only the business but also the respect of their peers. After leaving Hogwarts, Fred and George establish Weasleys' Wizard Wheezes in Diagon Alley, where their products are so popular the store is frequently too crowded to see the shelves.

THE DARK ARTS

Like most schools, Hogwarts subjects range from incredibly exciting to mind-numbingly boring, depending on one's preferences. There are, however, dangerous subjects that aren't taught at the school, nearly all of which fall under the Dark Arts.

Since most of the school's founders disagreed that the subject ought to be taught, Hogwarts students learn nothing in the way of practicing Dark magic, only how to defend against it. This stands in contrast to a school like Durmstrang, where Dark magic is said to be incorporated into the curriculum. To keep Hogwarts students from learning about this field of magic, the school requires permission slips to access the Restricted Section of the library, where such titles likely reside. Independent browsing is not allowed—the librarian fetches books on a reader's behalf. Most of the books in the Restricted Section are likely designed to be used by N.E.W.T.-level Defense Against the Dark Arts students who need more information on advanced Dark magic threats, especially if they are interested in pursuing a career as an Auror. It's safe to say these books are not kept in the library with the intent to educate students on how to practice Dark magic but rather serve as a means for them to know what they might encounter outside of school.

Secrets of the Darkest Art, the book Tom Riddle used to research the process of making Horcruxes, was most likely kept in the Restricted Section before Dumbledore had it removed. After Hermione uses a Summoning Charm to acquire the book from Albus Dumbledore's office following his funeral, she discovers it provides precise instructions on how to create a Horcrux. In the end, the trio consults its pages to determine how to destroy Voldemort's cursed items.

Potions, another compulsory subject at Hogwarts for the first five years alongside Defense Against the Dark Arts, teaches students how to make some potent and dangerous brews, but some potions are expressly forbidden, such as love potions and likely Polyjuice Potion. Despite the fact that students are probably not permitted to craft this draught, the recipe can be found in a book titled *Moste Potente Potions* from the Restricted Section. Naturally, some students find workarounds to the rules. During the 1992–1993 school year, Hermione tricks Gilderoy Lockhart into giving her a signed permission slip so she can borrow the book and use it to transform into Slytherin student Millicent Bulstrode, a plan that backfires terribly. It's also very likely the Restricted Section contains books detailing how to craft other forbidden brews.

While it's never expressly stated, it's probable that every subject offered at Hogwarts has a Dark counterpart that professors aren't permitted to teach. The Restricted Section could contain information on how to grow deadly plants, master harmful charms, jinxes and hexes or even use transfigurations in despicable ways. It would certainly explain why Madam Pince runs such a tight ship when it comes to protecting Hogwarts's books.

Hogwarts keeps its students from practicing Dark magic until the 1997–1998 school year, when Death Eaters infiltrate Hogwarts and run the institution. Death Eater Amycus Carrow takes over the teaching of Defense Against the Dark Arts, renaming the class simply Dark Arts. Carrow instructs students to cast the Unforgivable Curses and use the Cruciatus Curse on fellow students who had earned detentions. After Voldemort is killed in 1998 and Death Eaters like Carrow are sent to Azkaban, the class resumes its original purpose.

THE CREATION OF HORCRUXES

Horcrux magic is incredibly Dark and is considered taboo in the wizarding community, so it's no surprise most students at Hogwarts are blissfully unaware of its existence. This type of magic is incredibly advanced and can likely only be performed by the most powerful Dark witches and wizards, mainly because it serves as a means to cheat or at least evade death, something magic technically cannot do outright. Horcrux magic offers somewhat of a loophole, allowing the caster to prevent their own death by shattering their soul. Doing this successfully can help them stay alive even when, by all natural means, they should be dead.

Creating a Horcrux is a terrible and complex undertaking. The caster essentially binds a piece of their soul to an object so that when they die, that piece of their soul continues to live. In order to initiate this horrifying process, one must commit murder. This vile act splits the soul apart, an essential step in the process of creating a Horcrux. Then, the caster would need to trap that piece of their soul in an object of their choosing. Perhaps owing to how few people have achieved this, the exact method of how this is done is likely known only to those who've read Secrets of the Darkest Art.

It's likely that the difficulty of creating Horcruxes largely depends on the person's character, just as performing Unforgivable Curses is easier for those who have no morals. To someone like Lord Voldemort, killing is second nature. For an individual who has no desire to take another's life, the process would be much more difficult, and they'd likely fail (of course, they likely wouldn't dream of attempting the process in the first place). Other than Lord Voldemort, the only wizard known to have created a Horcrux is Herpo the Foul, an ancient Greek Dark wizard who created the first one, though it's likely others have since tried and may have succeeded. Lord Voldemort, who created seven, is the only wizard known to have created multiple.

While Horcruxes might seem like the perfect antidote to death for Dark witches and wizards, this type of magic comes with a price. Since you have to split your soul, it becomes unstable, and if your body is destroyed, as happens with Voldemort when he tries to kill Harry, you are left to simply exist in an incorporeal form, invisible to the rest of the world, less than even a ghost. Professor Slughorn mentions that death would be preferable to existing in such a state.

NECROMANCY

Necromancy is a branch of Dark magic that is used to raise the dead. Of course, thanks to natural limitations of magic, necromancy doesn't permit the raised person to fully come back to life. One example of necromancy at work is an Inferius, a dead body that has been reanimated with Dark magic. It does whatever its master asks of it and technically cannot be killed because it's already dead. Only fire can destroy an Inferius.

Inferi can be cursed to respond a certain way when disturbed. Voldemort has an army of Inferi stashed away in the lake surrounding his locket Horcrux. They are enchanted to awaken when anyone touches the surface of the water, which is what Harry does to collect water for Dumbledore when the latter drinks the cursed potion in which a Horcrux is supposedly hidden. The Inferi attack Harry, dragging him toward the water, and no spell Harry uses has any effect on them. The Inferi nearly pull Harry to the bottom of the lake until Dumbledore manages to drive them off with fire.

KNOWN ANNOTATIONS BY THE HALF-BLOOD PRINCE

During his time at Hogwarts, Snape heavily annotated his copy of *Advanced Potion-Making*. The textbook itself is used by students in N.E.W.T.-level Potions.

- For the **Draught of Living Death**, Snape advises crushing the sopophorous bean with the flat side of a silver dagger. Doing so, he writes, releases the bean's juice better than simply cutting it. He also suggests adding one clockwise stir after seven counterclockwise stirs. This will speed up the process of achieving a clear color.
- Snape's notes heavily altered the **Elixir to Induce Euphoria**, although it is unclear in what way, other than that he recommends adding a sprig of peppermint to counter unwanted side effects such as "excessive singing" and "nose-tweaking."
- As a one-step solution for a **poison antidote**, Snape suggests shoving a bezoar—specifically one taken from the stomach of a goat—down the throat of the poisoned individual. A bezoar is a stone-like mass of indigestible material (typically hair or other fibers) that forms in the digestive tract. According to Slughorn, bezoars are rare enough that it is important to know other antidotes in case one is not available. Snape did not appear to know or care about the bezoar's rarity when making this note.

The use of Inferi is a clever tool for Dark wizards. Collected in great enough numbers, these animated corpses can form an almost indestructible army that will do whatever their master requires. Since they have no mind of their own, they possess neither concern for their well-being and nor an ethical code. Creating Inferi likely requires intricate Dark magic, unlike the usual spells witches and wizards use to animate everyday objects.

Students at Hogwarts learn about Inferi in Defense Against the Dark Arts, but only how to defend against and destroy them as opposed to create them. In the 1996–1997 school year, Professor Severus Snape teaches his sixth-year students about Inferi, showing them the bloody remains of a person killed by these vile creatures.

UNFORGIVABLE CURSES

There's a reason three particular curses are labeled unforgivable: These spells can take away a person's free will, torture them or kill them. Casting one of these curses is considered a one-way ticket to Azkaban.

The three Unforgivable Curses are the Imperius Curse, the Cruciatus Curse and the Killing Curse. Students at Hogwarts learn how to defend themselves against these curses in their sixth year (although Harry's class learns about them during his fourth year). They are not taught how to cast them.

Not just anyone can cast these curses—those who are morally bankrupt have an easier time managing them than those who have a conscience. For instance, when Harry tries to cast the Cruciatus Curse on Bellatrix Lestrange after she murders Sirius Black in 1996, he fails despite the fact that he is blinded by fury. That gives a clear indication of just how challenging these spells are when you don't genuinely possess bad intentions.

Voldemort and his Death Eaters use these curses freely during his reign. In fact, Bellatrix Lestrange employs it to torture Neville's parents to the brink of insanity, and Voldemort casts the Killing Curse on Harry more than once.

CURSING OR BEWITCHING MUGGLE OBJECTS

Under no circumstances are wizards allowed to cast any sort of spell on Muggle objects that might cause them to perform any function other than their express purpose (except when these objects are authorized by the Ministry of Magic to be used as Portkeys). This is because these items typically make their way back into Muggle hands, to catastrophic consequences. The Ministry of Magic takes this offense seriously and dedicates an entire department to confiscating Muggle objects that have been cursed or bewitched (see pg. 148).

UNDERAGE MAGIC

Underage magic refers to any magic performed outside of Hogwarts by witches and wizards under the age of 17. Deliberately performing magic in front of Muggles or in a Muggle area is strictly forbidden. The use of underage magic is governed by the Decree for the Reasonable Restriction of Underage Sorcery, which the Ministry of Magic implemented in 1875.

Shortly after Hagrid introduces Harry to the magical community, he warns him that he is not allowed to use magic outside of school, "except in very special circumstances." These "special circumstances" fall under Clause 7 of the Decree for the Reasonable Restriction of Underage Sorcery, which states that magic may be used in the presence of Muggles in life-threatening situations (e.g., when Harry defends himself and Dudley from the Dementors in Little Whinging in 1995).

Underage wizards who violate this Decree typically receive a warning. Continued disregard for this law usually ends in immediate expulsion from Hogwarts, after which a Ministry official breaks your wand in two. In special cases, such as Harry's aforementioned run-in with Dementors, a hearing is arranged to decide the student's fate.

Wizards who are too young to attend Hogwarts are usually exempt from this law, simply because they cannot yet control their magical abilities and don't own a wand. Harry has a few of these accidents before he even knows he is a wizard: He regrows his hair every time Aunt Petunia cuts it, flies onto his Muggle school's roof to get away from Dudley and his friends and even unknowingly makes the glass vanish at the reptile house, causing the boa constrictor to escape. None of these incidents are held against him because he is not yet a student at Hogwarts.

Prior to the start of his second year at Hogwarts, Harry receives his first warning from the Ministry of Magic after Dobby the house-elf uses a Hovering Charm to drop Aunt Petunia's pudding onto the kitchen floor, causing a whipped cream explosion in front of her dinner guests. It appears the Ministry's tracking methods don't account for house-elves performing magic in the vicinity of an underage wizard. Harry is once again in trouble with the law when he accidentally blows up his Aunt Marge in 1993 but is given a pass when the Ministry recognizes the act as an unplanned loss of self-control. When he performs the Patronus Charm in 1995 to protect himself and Dudley from the Dementors, however, Harry is expelled. Thankfully, after the intervention of Albus Dumbledore, he gets to explain what happened during a hearing at the Ministry of Magic and is allowed to attend school after all.

In order to maintain the Statute of Secrecy, adult wizards are only permitted to perform magic in the presence of Muggles when absolutely necessary. In rare cases where wizards have no other choice but to resort to employing magic, such as in self-defense, the Ministry of Magic sends a team of Obliviators to modify any memories from the Muggle witnesses. The Muggle Protection Act ensures that the wizarding world remains a secret and that Muggles are kept safe from magic.

About the Authors

MuggleNet, the #1 Wizarding World Resource Since 1999, is dedicated to honoring the magic of the wizarding community by providing reliable, fun, informative content to our readers. The site is run by *Potter* aficionados who are passionate about making MuggleNet the best it can be. We take pride in our diverse group of 100+ global volunteers, ranging from teens to retirees.

A special acknowledgment to Felicia Grady and Kat Miller, the continuity editor and creative director of MuggleNet, respectively, for providing support, insight and feedback, as well as for planning and coordinating this project with the publisher and the incredible MuggleNet staff.

JENNIFER FANCHER is a Hufflepuff who's been a member of the MuggleNet editorial team since 2019. She lives near Chicago with her husband and their dog, Luna. While writing this book, she was also preparing to welcome her first child.

AMY HOGAN is a Hufflepuff, creative media manager for MuggleNet and producer/host of *SpeakBeasty: A Fantastic Beasts Podcast*. Her cat, Luna, contributed to this book with more than one keyboard nap.

MARICA LAING is a Gryffindor hailing from South Africa. She's a full-time freelance writer and volunteers at MuggleNet as a journalist and newsletter specialist. When she's not writing, she spends her time reading, making music and drinking copious amounts of tea.

MARISSA OSMAN is an author and academic who enjoys any chance to combine her creative and intellectual pursuits. Shortly after finishing her graduate degree at King's College London, Marissa coauthored MuggleNet's *Character Compendium* and *Hogwarts Handbook*. Unsurprisingly, she is a Ravenclaw.

LIZ YOUNG is a Ravenclaw, the marketing director at MuggleNet and part of the social media team for *SpeakBeasty: A Fantastic Beasts Podcast*. In her Muggle life, she uses her master's degree in anthropology to explore how entertainment and culture intersect.

Media Lab Books
For inquiries, call 646-449-8614

Copyright 2023 Topix Media Lab

Published by Topix Media Lab
14 Wall Street, Suite 3C
New York, NY 10005

Printed in China

All rights reserved. No part of this book may be reproduced in any form or by any electronic or mechanical means, including information storage and retrieval systems, without permission in writing from the publisher, except by a reviewer, who may quote brief passages in a review.

Certain photographs used in this publication are used by license or permission from the owner thereof, or are otherwise publicly available. This publication is not endorsed by any person or entity appearing herein. Any product names, logos, brands or trademarks featured or referred to in the publication are the property of their respective trademark owners. Media Lab Books is not affiliated with, nor sponsored or endorsed by, any of the persons, entities, product names, logos, brands or other trademarks featured or referred to in any of its publications.

ISBN-13: 978-1-956403-26-8
ISBN-10: 1-956403-26-4

CEO Tony Romando

Vice President & Publisher Phil Sexton
Senior Vice President of Sales & New Markets Tom Mifsud
Vice President of Retail Sales & Logistics Linda Greenblatt
Chief Financial Officer Vandana Patel
Manufacturing Director Nancy Puskuldjian
Digital Marketing & Strategy Manager Elyse Gregov

Chief Content Officer Jeff Ashworth
Director of Editorial Operations Courtney Kerrigan
Senior Acquisitions Editor Noreen Henson
Creative Director Susan Dazzo
Photo Director Dave Weiss
Executive Editor Tim Baker

Content Editor Juliana Sharaf
Content Designer Alyssa Bredin Quirós
Features Editor Trevor Courneen
Assistant Managing Editor Tara Sherman
Designers Glen Karpowich, Mikio Sakai
Copy Editor & Fact Checker Madeline Raynor
Assistant Photo Editor Jenna Addesso
Contributing Editor Felicia Grady

Cover art and all interior art: Shutterstock

Additional fact-checking and research: Catherine Lai

1C-B23-1